Love's power to forgive
is stronger than hate's
power to get even.

—An Amish Proverb

SUGARCREEK AMISH MYSTERIES

HOME SWEET
Sugarcreek

ELIZABETH LUDWIG

Guideposts
New York

Sugarcreek Amish Mysteries is a trademark of Guideposts.

Published by Guideposts Books & Inspirational Media
110 William Street
New York, NY 10038

Guideposts.org

Cover and interior design by Müllerhaus
Cover illustration by Bill Bruning, represented by Deborah Wolfe, LTD.
Typeset by Aptara, Inc.

Printed and bound in the United States of America
10 9 8 7 6 5 4 3 2

To Abby and Derrick:

I'm so proud of your hard work and dedication to each other and to your family. You're building a home...laying each brick with love, patience, gentleness, and self-control. Best of all, you've trusted in a foundation of faith and hope in the One Who brought you together.
May your home always be blessed.

CHAPTER ONE

S un, smoke, and the sweet scent of late summer squash tickled Cheryl's nose as she mounted the steps of the Friendship Mennonite Church. Here and there, brightly colored leaves dotted the pavement until a playful breeze sent them skittering down the walk.

Ah, fall!

It was such a pleasant time of year, especially here in Sugarcreek, where people relished the sights and savored the distinct flavors of the season. She paused with her hand on the door and inhaled until her lungs felt near to bursting. Columbus had never smelled this way—never so full of promise and thanksgiving.

And farmland. And cows. She grimaced wryly. Country living meant the occasional country fragrance, but even that minor irritation couldn't dampen her spirits today.

As if to remind her of the time, the same cheerful wind swirled up the steps and fluttered the hem of her skirt. It wasn't a plain dress, like a few of the older members of this congregation wore, but since a larger number preferred modest English attire, she felt right at home.

Cheryl scurried through the heavy glass doors on a gust of crisp November air.

"Good morning, Cheryl." One of the deacons, Dwight Foster, greeted her at the entrance to the sanctuary.

"Hi, Dwight." She rubbed her hands lightly over her arms. "It's nippy out there. Bet we'll have some snowy days soon."

His head bobbed in agreement. "Most likely. We'll be digging out the hats and scarves. I have a very nice one that Suzy gave me for Christmas last year."

She smiled as she took the bulletin he extended and tucked it into the pages of her Bible. "Am I late?"

"Not yet. Singing hasn't even started." His right hand rose to tug at a lock of graying hair that fell perpetually over his brow. "Say, if you're not busy after church, would you mind sticking around for a few minutes? Suzy and I have a project we'd like to talk to you about."

Thinking of Suzy's cheerful face widened the smile on Cheryl's lips. "Sure. I'll look for you once the service is over."

"Wonderful. Thank you, Cheryl."

Dwight gave one final nod in her direction and then turned to welcome more latecomers. At least she wasn't the last, Cheryl thought as she hurried to a seat near the back. Not that anyone would have minded. Here at Friendship Mennonite, people paid less attention to the time you arrived and more to the fact that you came. It was one of the things she loved about this church. The conservative teaching also made her feel less of an outsider amongst her Amish friends. With her relationship to the Millers deepening, she felt this was important, though she wouldn't venture to guess why that might be so.

While Cheryl still attended Silo church often and especially enjoyed their contemporary music and the excitement a "mega-size" church generated, she found herself drawn more and more to the smaller church of Friendship Mennonite. She felt at home here, like she was among family.

Setting aside her thoughts, Cheryl focused on losing herself to the music and the preaching that followed. When the last "amen" echoed off the walls, she not only felt refreshed, she felt excited. And challenged. Pastor Lory's preaching had a way of reaching deep into her heart and planting seeds, just like the farmers around Sugarcreek did with freshly turned soil. Today's teaching on the characteristics of sacrificial love was a timely message, one that had struck an especially tender chord considering the conversation she'd just had with Levi.

Thinking of him stirred an ache in Cheryl's heart. She gathered her things, anxious to find Dwight and Suzy now that the service was over. What could they want to speak to her about? Dwight served the church in several capacities, but most were connected to the building and grounds. If they knew anything about her skill with a hammer, they wouldn't be seeking her help for that, so…

Fear turned her stomach sour. Was Pastor Lory thinking of retiring? Granted, God didn't want His people following after men, but she had only recently joined the church. She enjoyed the atmosphere of faith and family, and to lose their pastor…

Cheryl felt a bump from behind and clutched her purse and Bible tighter to her chest.

"Beg your pardon, Miss Cooper."

The softly mumbled words could only come from one source. Cheryl turned and looked up into the grime-encrusted, bearded face of the drifter known about town only as "Muddy."

"My fault, Muddy. I was in a hurry. I didn't see you."

He didn't meet her eyes, but Cheryl thought she saw a hint of a wry smile behind the scraggly gray beard.

"No worries. Most people don't."

He turned, his angular shoulders jutting beneath the ragged folds of his dingy yellow shirt. A T-shirt, she corrected mentally. One in need of patches. Where was his coat? Hadn't she remarked on the nip in the air only an hour ago? How could he stand it?

She shifted her purse to one arm. "Uh...Muddy?"

"Yeah?"

She chewed her lip. Though she tried to look past the grime, he refused to meet her eyes, which either left her staring at the dirt creasing his neck or the stains covering his T-shirt.

"Um..." She stepped closer and lowered her voice. "It'll be getting cold soon. Do you need a coat? I could get you one from the clothing closet."

Clearly made uncomfortable by her question, Muddy shuffled from foot to foot, his jagged fingernails making a rasping sound across his scruffy cheek. "A coat?"

"It'll only take me a minute." She ran her gaze over his lanky form. He was definitely skinny, and age had added a stoop to his shoulders, but at one time, he'd probably cut an impressive figure. "I'd say you're about a men's large?"

"About that," he muttered. His head lowered, and he cast his gaze from side to side. "You really don't need to bother, Miss Cooper. I only came by today to pick up something from the office."

Something about his posture spoke to Cheryl's heart and reminded her of their pastor's words only a short time ago. She laid her hand over his forearm and pasted on a bright smile. "It's no trouble, Muddy. I'll be right back, okay?"

At his nod, she set off in the direction of the clothing closet. It took her a moment to wade through the people lingering outside the sanctuary, several of whom wanted to chat, but Cheryl finally made her way downstairs. The clothing closet was where the church kept items to be used in cases of emergency—things like home fires, flooding or other natural disasters, and sometimes more personal crises, like an unplanned pregnancy or domestic violence. Though this wasn't one of those situations, the closet was open to anyone in the community, and Cheryl knew no one would object to caring for the homeless.

She checked the inventory chart taped to the door, found an item she thought would fit, and then marked through the list so that no one else came looking for a coat that was no longer in the closet. Draping her prize over her arm, Cheryl made her way back upstairs, but instead of finding Muddy, she ran into Dwight and Suzy Foster.

"Cheryl, there you are. We thought you'd left," Suzy said, her blue eyes twinkling.

For just a moment, Cheryl felt a twinge of astonishment.

Suzy was battling cancer.

As swiftly as it came, the emotion fled. Suzy loved the Lord and trusted in His care. It shouldn't surprise her or anyone else that she walked around with a look of pure joy on her face.

"I didn't forget." Cheryl held up the collar of the coat and checked the hallway. "Anybody see which way Muddy went?"

Dwight draped his arm protectively around his wife. "Muddy's here?"

"Dwight," Suzy chided with a gentle poke to her husband's ribs, "he's harmless."

Dwight grinned and rubbed his side. "What? I didn't see him come in, that's all."

Suzy's gaze drifted to the coat. "Is that for him?"

Cheryl nodded and tucked the garment back over her arm. "Yeah. I thought he might need it with the weather turning colder. I can get it to him another time, I suppose."

Dwight's answering nod came almost too quickly. "Good idea. So about that thing we wanted to ask you...are you free for lunch? I thought we could talk over sandwiches."

Cheryl's stomach rumbled in reply.

Suzy laughed. "Our house sound okay?"

"I'm cooking," Dwight volunteered.

"It's sliced turkey on bread," Suzy scolded.

He turned with a sly grin and handed Cheryl a slip of paper. "Here's the address. Will you need directions?"

"Nope." She pulled her phone from her purse. "I'll enter it into my navigation."

"Good. Then we'll see you in a little bit," Suzy said, turning for the door. Before she got there, Dwight scurried ahead to hold it open then wrapped his arm lovingly around his wife's waist as he guided her through the parking lot. When they reached the car, he opened the door and assisted her inside.

The drive to the Fosters' home was short but pretty with so many of the trees lining the road clinging to their fall colors. A good stiff wind would shake the leaves loose, but for now, Cheryl rolled down her window an inch and enjoyed the cool air. When she pulled into the Fosters' driveway, Dwight waited for her on an expansive wraparound porch. Their house was a single-story plantation that looked like it belonged more along the banks of the Mississippi than in rural Sugarcreek, yet it seemed fitting for the Fosters.

Dwight lifted his hand in greeting. "Welcome, Cheryl. You found the place okay?"

"No problem," she said as she climbed from her car.

"Good." He waited until she joined him on the porch then reached for the handle on the tall glass door, but he looked hesitant about going inside.

"Everything okay, Dwight?" Cheryl asked.

He frowned and took his hand off the knob. "Listen, about lunch...I'm sorry it couldn't be anything more fancy than plain old sandwiches. I've taken over most of the cooking since Suzy took ill, and, well"—his cheeks colored, and he pushed his hands into his pockets—"my culinary expertise doesn't exactly match hers."

Cheryl gave his shoulder a sympathetic pat. "Don't worry about a thing. Your cooking has to be better than mine anyway."

His smile turned teasing. "Oh yeah?"

She held up one hand. "I tried cooking a turkey last Thanksgiving. Let's just say I still haven't managed to live it down.

How was I supposed to know I had to look in both ends of the turkey for the giblets?"

He laughed and led her inside, where Suzy greeted them in the hall. Though her cheeks bore a pale sheen, her eyes were twinkling and bright, and she waved for them to join her in the dining room.

"Cheryl, come in. Thank you so much for agreeing to meet with us."

"It's my pleasure, Suzy."

She let her gaze roam the buttery yellow walls and crisp white moldings that topped them. In one corner of the room stood an antique curio cabinet filled with blue pottery. Scattered amid the pottery were wedding photos, yellowed with age but still beautiful. Cheryl smiled at one of Dwight with his chin resting atop Suzy's head, their hands clasped around a cake knife.

Opposite the dining room was an old-fashioned parlor, replete with beaded lamps and a small piano.

Cheryl breathed an appreciative sigh. "I love your home."

"Thank you," Suzy said, blushing graciously.

"Do you play?"

She pointed to the piano tucked into the corner. Sheet music had been left open on the music rack, but surprisingly, Suzy shook her head.

"Not anymore. I hope to get back to it someday, but for now…"

She trailed off, and Dwight quickly stepped in by sweeping his hand toward the dining room table. "Shall we sit down?"

"Sure. Thank you, Dwight." Cheryl set her purse on the floor and slid out of her coat. "So what is this about? I figured it had something to do with the church."

Dwight took Cheryl's coat and shook his head. "Not this time. Well, not exactly. Not about the church building, anyway. This is about the Church History Celebration. You heard we've been working on it, right?"

"I heard about the celebration. I didn't realize you were on the committee."

His lips curled in a wry grin. "Gotta have something to fill my time."

Suzy patted his arm affectionately. "You'd think he would enjoy his retirement more after finally laying down his tool belt."

Cheryl smiled. "You miss building furniture?"

Dwight shrugged, and his fingers rose to tug his eyebrow. "Not the job so much." He cast a furtive, almost embarrassed glance at his wife. "I miss the smell of wood and sawdust now and again, I suppose. But I'm where I'm supposed to be. That's all that matters."

Suzy dropped her gaze and said nothing, but Cheryl knew the conversation made her uncomfortable. It was no secret Dwight had chosen an early retirement so he could be with his wife while she underwent cancer treatments.

"So about the celebration?" Cheryl prompted.

"Right."

Dwight indicated one of the chairs for Cheryl then circled around to pull out a chair for Suzy. She had already laid out plates, cups, and silverware. At the center of the table sat a tray with sliced turkey, fresh lettuce and tomato, plus several slices of wheat bread.

Dwight sat, and after saying a quick grace, he handed Cheryl the tray of sandwich meat then grabbed his napkin and began tearing at the edges.

"I'm kind of excited about the celebration actually. Suzy came up with a great idea for incorporating a bit of the local traditions." His gaze switched to his wife. "You want to tell her about it?"

Suzy leaned forward, excitement that matched her husband's sparking in her gaze. "You see, Cheryl, the whole purpose behind a Church History Celebration is to celebrate our roots—all of which are deeply embedded in Sugarcreek. But as we began making plans, we realized this wasn't just about our history. We wanted to do something for the local residents of our community—help them understand where we came from and teach them how the town began."

"For instance, did you know Sugarcreek used to be called Shanesville?" Dwight blurted. His head bobbed once then twice in rapid succession. "I read all about it in the town charter."

"Well, I..."

"It sort of just sprang up out in the middle of nowhere."

"At the point where two Indian trails met," Cheryl said.

His eyebrows rose in surprise. "That's right. How did...?"

"Pam told me. The librarian over at the Sugarcreek Public Library," Cheryl continued when Dwight appeared confused.

She put the finishing touches on her sandwich, pressed on the top piece of bread, and took a bite.

Suzy's voice rose hopefully. "So you've already done a bit of research on the town's history?"

The sudden chiming of an ornate grandfather clock gave Cheryl the time she needed to swallow. When it finished, she shook her head. "Not exactly. I just happen to have a knack for remembering details." Something she'd come to recognize about herself since moving to Sugarcreek. "Though I have to admit, I really do find these historical tidbits interesting."

"See, Suzy? I told you. I knew she'd be perfect for the job." Dwight's face flushed with excitement. He dropped his sandwich on to his plate, scattering crumbs over the edge on to the table.

"Hold on, dear. We haven't even asked her yet."

"Asked me what? What is all this about?"

Suzy laid her hand on her husband's arm. He, in turn, nodded for her to explain. She turned to Cheryl. "We're thinking about putting together a diorama for the celebration—a three-dimensional display, if you will—depicting *all* of the town's history, beginning with its earliest days right up to the way it looks today. This would of course include a section on the impact of the local churches. That led us to think of ways we could incorporate it into things the town is already doing."

"Like the Swiss Festival?" Cheryl asked.

"Exactly," Dwight said. "I've already talked to the mayor. He thinks combining the church history project with the annual Swiss Festival is an excellent idea. He suggested setting it up at Village Hall. People could walk through as part of their festival experience."

"Sounds like a lot of work." None of which Cheryl felt qualified to tackle. She leaned back against her chair and crossed her arms. "I mean, it sounds neat, and I think people would really like learning about the town's history..."

"Not just the town's history," Dwight said. "Their own. We're thinking about including a section on the town's founders...you know...the original settlers."

"Pioneers," Cheryl said.

"Exactly."

Cheryl gave a slow nod. "That will definitely draw interest. Digging into one's ancestry is very popular right now."

"So you think it's a good idea?" Suzy asked, her nervous fidgeting suddenly matching Dwight's.

"I think it's a wonderful idea. What I don't understand is what part I play in all of this."

"That's simple." Dwight's grin widened as he looked first to his wife and then to Cheryl. Leaning forward, he fixed her with an earnest stare that sparked an uneasy rolling in the pit of Cheryl's stomach. "The church history project is all your uncle's idea."

"But...th-that's impossible," Cheryl stammered.

Her hands bunched into clammy fists. This was all wrong! Her uncle couldn't have come up with the idea for the church history project. He couldn't because...

Her uncle was dead.

CHAPTER TWO

It had been a long time since Cheryl felt the dull ache in her chest associated with her uncle Ralph. Five years, in fact...the last of which she'd spent living in Sugarcreek. Gone was the hungry rumbling in her belly caused by the delicious scent of fresh bread wafting from her plate. Gone too was the excitement she'd felt on hearing about the idea of a history project for the celebration.

Cheryl swallowed the lump that pushed up in her throat and sat up straighter in her chair. If she were honest, it was her uncle's passing that had brought her to Sugarcreek in the first place. Aunt Mitzi would never have volunteered to serve as a missionary to Papua New Guinea otherwise.

She framed her words carefully. "Uncle Ralph wasn't a Mennonite. Besides, he's been gone a long time now. He couldn't have..."

Suzy's eyes rounded, and she put up her hand hastily. "No, no...I'm sorry. That didn't come out right at all. Dwight?" She looked imploringly at her husband.

He cleared his throat. "You see, Cheryl, several years ago, while your uncle Ralph was still alive, he and I talked about putting together a celebration just like the one we're planning now. In fact, he even looked into organizing the event, which really surprised me considering how he mostly liked keeping to himself. But he was really into the idea, you know? He drew up some plans, started talking to vendors…but then he got sick and, well, things sort of got put on hold."

"Your uncle loved this town, Cheryl." Suzy pushed aside her plate, her sandwich as yet untouched, and reached out to clasp Cheryl's hand. "He loved the people here and wanted to give them something they could be proud of for generations to come. Plus, he was such a history buff. I have no doubt he has some items stashed away somewhere that we could use for the project. That's why we thought of you when we started talking about adding the diorama of the town's history to the Swiss Festival. The entire thing would be as much a memorial to him as it is to Sugarcreek."

A memorial in honor of Uncle Ralph? Warmth flooded Cheryl's heart. Every memory she had of her uncle was connected to this town. Granted, the festival wasn't specifically about him, but she had no doubt he would have supported a history project like the one Dwight and Suzy talked about.

Suzy's gaze bounced from Cheryl to her husband and back again. "If you'd like some time to think about it…"

Cheryl couldn't help the smile that spread across her face. She leaned forward and braced both elbows on the table. "I don't need to think. It's a wonderful idea, one I know Uncle Ralph would have loved. I'd be honored to be a part of it."

As if to celebrate her announcement, Dwight picked up his sandwich and held it aloft. The lettuce flapped like a flag, but completely unperturbed, he toasted the town history project then took a hearty bite. Cheryl laughed, and then the three of them spent the next hour chatting about their ideas for the project in between bites of turkey and sips of Coke.

"Now we'll need to put together some kind of committee to help with the technical side of things—the building of the dioramas and so forth." Dwight swiped his napkin over his mouth and pushed his empty plate aside. "I'll be more than happy to handle those things if you'd be willing to tackle the hard stuff."

Cheryl paused with her glass in midair. "The hard stuff?"

"He means the research." Suzy leaned playfully into her husband's shoulder. "Old Dwight here never could get a handle on Google."

"Now, Suzy, you know you can't teach an old dog new tricks."

They laughed together, the sound a pleasant mix of love and teasing. After a moment, Dwight's hand rose to stroke his wife's cheek. It was a sweet gesture, one that made Cheryl ponder the importance of their marriage vows, particularly the part about "in sickness and in health." For both their sakes, she prayed it was more health than sickness.

And then, like an unexpected gust of wind, Cheryl's thoughts blew to Levi. He was a man who could be counted on to keep his word, only in this case, it wasn't a vow of marriage—it was a promise that would forever keep them from marriage.

Unless God showed them a different path, she reminded herself sternly.

Not wishing to be caught staring, she lowered her gaze then grabbed her napkin, bunched it into a ball, and dropped it on to her plate. Grabbing her glass, she moved to rise, but Dwight claimed his plate and hers before Cheryl could.

"I'll get the dishes."

"Oh, that's not necessary," Cheryl said, but Dwight gave an adamant shake of his head.

"No trouble. Right, honey?"

Suzy nodded. "Treating you to lunch was the least we could do. After all, it's not like we can compensate you for the time you're going to spend researching the town's history."

Cheryl smiled and pressed her glass into Dwight's hand. "Like I said earlier, I actually enjoy picking up a few historical tidbits here and there. This ought to be fun."

But the next afternoon, as she made the walk home after a busy day at work, Cheryl was less certain. While she enjoyed history, it had never been her strong suit. What did she really know about Sugarcreek other than the little she'd learned living here? Could she do a reasonable job representing *all* of the town's residents, including the Amish and Mennonite ones?

On that score, she knew just where to turn for help. Her best friend, Naomi Miller, was Amish and would likely be a fountain of information when it came to researching the town's Plain settlers. And it was early yet, just after five. More than likely, she wouldn't run into Levi since the hours on a working farm often stretched until well after sundown.

Making a snap decision, she climbed into her car instead of going inside the house then tapped the steering wheel impatiently.

Her fingers itched for a keyboard so she could start Googling Sugarcreek's history, but before she did that, she had probably better check with Naomi about helping with the things she couldn't find online.

Cheryl pulled on to the road and then turned toward the Millers' farm. This time of year, the family had finished with the harvesting but the work to be done was still in full swing. Along with her normal chores, Naomi would be putting up jars of her famous apple butter. Cheryl could almost feel the cinnamon and cloves melting on her tongue as she passed through the covered bridge that opened to the Millers' land and farther on, their large white farmhouse.

Brightly painted maples waved as she wound up the road to the Millers'. She loved this season and was grateful the brilliant colors lingered into November this year. She rolled to a stop in the driveway then climbed out of the car and tarried a moment on the porch as she soaked in the sight and scent of the lovely fall flowers decorating the steps leading to the Millers' door.

"Hello, Cheryl. You are here to see *Maam*?"

Levi's deep voice sent a shock wave through her midsection. Somehow she kept her fingers from rising to her unruly hair as she turned. "Hi, Levi."

He stood with his feet firmly planted and his hands braced on his hips . . . as solid and handsome as the trees she'd been admiring on the drive up. Cheryl averted her gaze and managed a weak wave toward the door.

"As a matter of fact, I *was* looking for Naomi. Is she home?"

"She is home, but she is not inside. She is at the petting zoo helping close up for the winter."

Cheryl felt a small niggle of disappointment, which was quickly dispelled with Levi's next words.

"Shall I walk with you there?"

Much as she wanted to say yes, a walk was hardly conducive to the agreement they'd both made to keep from acting on their feelings for each other. She pushed her hands into the pockets of her jacket and shrugged. "You don't have to do that, Levi. Besides, I don't want to intrude if Naomi is busy."

"She is never too busy for you." His smile warmed, sending tingles clear down to her toes. "And it is no bother."

He extended his hand in the direction of the barns then gave a tilt of his head. "Come. She will be happy to see you."

So it was true. He did intend to keep his word about not letting their decision ruin their friendship. Could this day shine any brighter? Cheryl resisted the urge to skip down the stairs—which probably would have ended in disaster anyway—and fell into step alongside him.

"It's a beautiful afternoon, isn't it? I adore these fall temperatures. Makes me want to spend time outside."

Levi shot her a mischievous grin. "Is that so? I am sure I could find you a job here on the farm if you like." He scratched his temple as though deep in thought. "Shearing will be coming up in the spring. Maybe we could make a lamber of you."

Cheryl laughed. "I was thinking more along the lines of long walks by the pond."

She froze as soon as she uttered the words. What on earth had made her say such a thing? Now he'd think she was going back on their agreement and was openly flirting with him.

His answering chuckle made her fuzzy with relief inside. "Indeed. Well, long walks by the pond do not sound so bad either." He pointed toward the pasture where several horses munched contentedly on grass. "Ranger misses you. I am certain he would not mind a walk."

As if he'd heard his name, the black gelding lifted his head and pranced closer to the fence.

"You will have to pet him now," Levi said. "I doubt he is going to let you pass without stopping to say hello."

Cheryl changed course but then paused before she reached the fence. "Oh, but I don't have..."

Before she could finish, Levi pulled an apple from a pocket in his coat and held it toward her.

She plucked it from his fingers with a smile. "If carrying apples in your pocket for Ranger is typical, I'm sure he hardly misses *me* at all."

She fed the apple to Ranger and watched as he munched loudly. "I'd say that's one horse who knows how to appreciate a good thing."

Levi leaned forward and rested his forearms atop the fence. "Perhaps it is because having known lack, he is more grateful for the gift. And the giver."

Something in his tone arrested Cheryl's thinking. She eyed him thoughtfully. He wasn't talking about Ranger or his previous owner. "Are you speaking from experience?"

He shrugged, but his enigmatic smile made her think perhaps he referred to her. She brushed off her hands. This time she couldn't resist running them through her hair. "Guess I'd better see about finding Naomi," she said, a trifle breathlessly.

If he noticed her nervous fidgeting, he didn't let on. He merely nodded and accompanied her the rest of the way to the petting zoo, where Naomi and the rest of the Miller children were busily cleaning stalls and repairing fences.

Upon catching sight of them, Esther, the youngest of the Millers' children, straightened and offered a vigorous wave. "Cheryl!"

Naomi set down the feed buckets she'd been stacking and crossed the yard, a welcoming smile on her lips. "What a surprise. We were not expecting you today."

"Sorry to drop by unannounced," Cheryl said.

"Friends do not need an invitation," Naomi said, wiping her hands on the apron covering her dress then smoothing out the wrinkles. "Besides, we were just about to take a break."

She looked over her shoulder at Elizabeth and Esther, who happily set aside their brooms and went to fetch a plate of cookies Cheryl spied sitting on a nearby workbench.

Naomi's gaze switched to Levi. "Son, go and fetch your brothers, *ja*? And your *daed* too. Let him know I have fresh cider to go with the cookies."

The Millers' cider was renowned in Sugarcreek, and Seth wouldn't be the only one looking forward to a glass. Cheryl's mouth watered at the thought of the icy sweetness on her tongue.

While Levi went to do his stepmother's bidding, Cheryl followed Naomi to a couple of barrels that had been overturned and a plank laid across them to serve as a table.

"So what is on your mind, Cheryl?" Naomi handed her a glass of cider and poured another for herself. "To what do we owe the pleasure?"

Cheryl held her glass aloft. "I would say it's the cider, but the truth is, I actually do have a reason. Have you got a minute?"

Naomi nodded and then listened as Cheryl explained her conversation with the Fosters and their idea to dedicate a project on the town's history for the Swiss Festival. When she finished, Naomi's eyes gleamed with interest.

"So what do you think?" Cheryl asked. "Could you help me gather some information on the town's first Amish settlers?"

"*Hmm.*" Her head tilted to one side. "I am not so sure I am the best person to ask."

"What?" Esther and Elizabeth asked in unison. They had stood silently by while Cheryl talked. Now they stared open-mouthed at their mother.

"Wh-what?" Cheryl repeated. She lowered her glass, momentarily made speechless by Naomi's reluctance. "Is it the farm? I know this is a busy time of year, but I..."

Naomi shook her head. "*Ne*, Cheryl, it is not that at all." Her gaze flicked to her daughters. "Of course I will make time to help if I can. The problem is my lack of knowledge." She looked at Cheryl once more. "I did not grow up here, remember? I moved after Seth and I were married."

Relief cleared the frown from Cheryl's lips. "That's no problem. I'm really not expecting you to do all of the research. I just need to know who to talk to. I thought maybe you could ask around, find someone who knows a little bit about the town's history, and I'll take it from there."

"You could speak to Daed," Esther said, her voice climbing with excitement.

"Ja," Elizabeth said. "He knows all there is to know about Sugarcreek, *ain't so,* Maam?"

Naomi smiled. "He knows much about the town's history, for sure and for certain."

A shadow fell in the doorway, and then Seth entered the barn, his knuckles rasping against his beard. "What is this? What do I know?"

Though she tried to keep her gaze from wandering past Seth, Cheryl couldn't help but notice that Levi had not accompanied him back.

"The history of Amish settlers in Sugarcreek," Naomi said. While Esther and Elizabeth passed out cookies and cider to the men, she went on to explain about Cheryl's project for the Swiss Festival. "So," she concluded, "we were wondering if you might be interested in helping out."

"It is an interesting project," Seth said, sounding a trifle doubtful. He fingered the rim of his glass and cast an almost apologetic glance at Cheryl. "Unfortunately, I am not certain I will have the time to devote to it. Naomi and I have discussed building a greenhouse, and I had thought to begin the work before the snow flies."

Disappointment surged through Cheryl. It looked like finding someone to help her with her Amish research was going to be harder than she thought.

"Perhaps I could help."

Cheryl jerked her head up at Levi's voice. He wasn't looking at her, however, but directed his words to his father. "The harvest is finished, so I will have some time before we need to get ready for spring. I am certain I could do some checking around, see if anyone would be willing to share old family records and such. That is, if Cheryl would not mind."

Working closely with him a couple of times a week? Riding with him while they spoke to neighbors and friends? No, she didn't mind.

For the first time, all gazes swung to fix on Cheryl, but it was Levi's gaze that weighed the heaviest. She swallowed past a sudden lump in her throat and nodded.

"Um…that would be wonderful, Levi. Thank you." She stifled the nervous fluttering in her stomach and feigned a careless shrug. "So long as I'm not pulling you away from anything, I would really appreciate the help."

"Well then, it is settled." Seth braced his hands on the makeshift table as he rose. "Caleb and Eli will help with the greenhouse, and Levi will help Cheryl with the history project. It is *goot*, ja?"

While the others broke into unrelated conversation, Cheryl risked a sidelong peek at Levi. To her surprise, their eyes met and held a full second before he looked away, suddenly caught up in the conversation between his dad and Caleb.

Cheryl's cheeks heated. Yes, she thought, sucking in a deep breath. As Seth would say, working with Levi would be very "goot" indeed.

Chapter Three

Many times throughout the next day, when she wasn't busy helping customers, Cheryl pondered the best way to tackle the town history project. It wasn't the research that bothered her. In the half hour she'd stolen during lunch, she'd pulled several articles and photos off the Internet. Putting the information together in a way that would do justice to her uncle Ralph and the town's founders was another matter entirely, and the responsibility weighed heavily on her shoulders.

The moment closing time arrived at the Swiss Miss, she flipped the sign and locked up then hurried out the door toward the public library. It was Tuesday, which meant the library hours extended later than normal. She'd be able to accomplish quite a bit of research before heading home for a late supper.

Located just off Main Street on Broadway, the Sugarcreek branch of the Tuscarawas County Library wasn't exactly easy walking distance. Still, Cheryl needed the exercise, and since she didn't want to waste any time by going home to fetch her car, she tugged her collar up around her ears and picked up her pace.

A quaint brick building housed the library, entirely unremarkable except for the scalloped trim adorning the eaves and the Swiss-inspired woodwork above the windows and door.

Cheryl had always liked the place but mainly because of what was inside. Rows upon rows of books greeted her as she stepped through the door, along with the sweet, spicy scent of simmering apple cider.

"Good afternoon, and welcome to the—oh, hello, Cheryl." Pam, the branch manager, cut her customary greeting short and offered a cheerful wave. "I got those books you asked for on Papua New Guinea. Heard any more from your aunt Mitzi?"

Cheryl waved back and then slid from her jacket. "Thank you, Pam. No, not yet. She's supposed to be out of touch for a while, but I'll let you know when I hear from her."

Pam paused from shelving books and motioned toward a table near the door. "We have hot spiced cider there, if you'd like a cup. 'Tis the season. Fall, I mean," she said with a wink before returning to the books.

It was indeed. Cheryl poured herself a cup and then carried it braced in both palms to a table near one of the windows. Several people browsed the aisles, many with some of Pam's cider in their hands. Cheryl set down her things and took a sip before turning to scowl at the many books that lined the walls.

"Something I can help you with?"

This time it was the library assistant, and not Pam, who spoke. Diminutive in stature, Violet Bechnel was an older Amish woman with a sweet-yet-serious demeanor that suited the library setting. At the moment, she peered unblinking at Cheryl through a pair of thick glasses.

"Are you looking for something in particular?" she asked, punctuating the question with a poke of her thumb over her shoulder.

"I am, actually," Cheryl replied and then proceeded to explain what she needed and why. Violet responded with an occasional nod.

"It all sounds very interesting," she said when Cheryl finished. "I'm sure we have a few things that could help. Have you thought about searching the courthouse archives?"

Cheryl nodded. "I have, but I figured I'd come here first, see what I could dig up using books and old newspaper articles."

"*Ach*, I see." The hem of Violet's plain dress fluttered as she crossed to an archaic-looking microfiche machine. "Research books are toward the back, but if you are looking for newspaper articles, I'm afraid you will have to start here. We haven't had the time or resources to switch everything to digital, at least not yet." She pointed to a long row of cabinets. "The microfilm is labeled by date. It will help if you know the time period you are looking for, although anything you find here will only go back fifty years or so."

Cheryl's shoulders drooped, and she stifled a groan. Searching through microfiche would take hours. On the bright side, at least she had a cup of warm cider to tide her over until supper.

"Okay. Thank you, Violet. I'll go ahead and get started."

"Let me know if you need anything," she said, already turning away to see whom she could help next.

Pulling out a chair, Cheryl tried not to wish for Google and prepared to sift through years of old newspapers. Once she got started, however, she found she enjoyed reading some of the old stories. In fact, a full two hours passed before the rumbling in her stomach reminded her that she needed to wrap up her research.

She leaned back in her chair and glanced at her watch. It was slightly after seven thirty. There was just enough time left to print out the articles she wanted before heading home. She gathered up her things then reached for the Off button on the microfiche when a tiny headline on the bottom of the page caught her eye:

Amish Man Declared Innocent after Informal Investigation

The title alone was enough to stir Cheryl's interest. The Amish people she knew were peaceful, law-abiding citizens. What charge could this man possibly have faced? She retook her seat and increased the size of the picture in order to read the entire article.

Police determined on Thursday that Datschel Watters played no part in the drowning death of his brother after an informal investigation that had many people questioning motives. Though no evidence was ever revealed to the contrary, Watters's claim that his brother's death was an accident raised enough eyebrows to spark the initial inquiry. Family members were unavailable to speak to reporters, but a friend close to the family remains steadfast in his belief of Watters's innocence and asked that the people of the community lay their suspicions aside to allow the family to grieve in peace.

It was the very last line of the article that arrested Cheryl's attention. Lay aside their suspicions? It was as though the reporter intentionally pronounced the case unsolved despite the police department's declaration. Weren't most drownings accidental? What had happened to cause such a startling investigation in the first place, and why had the man's innocence garnered so little coverage?

Despite the hour, Cheryl scrolled back several pages until she stumbled on another article with a similar headline:

Investigation Continues into Amish Man's Link to Brother's Untimely Death

The verbiage in this second article was similar to the first one she had read, but more interesting than the details were the quotes by local residents, several of whose surnames Cheryl recognized.

"They were known to be competitive," one person said. Cheryl stopped to reread the name—Robert Gleason. Bob Gleason? She checked the date on the article. No, Bob would have been too young. His father, perhaps? She settled deeper into her chair and kept reading.

Among his many other talents, Trampas Watters was known to be an avid swimmer. One member of the Sugarcreek community claimed he was good enough to be an Olympian, which made his drowning late Saturday evening even more suspicious to police. When questioned regarding the details of his brother's death, older brother Datschel simply replied, "No comment."

"Closing in fifteen minutes."

Violet's voice at Cheryl's elbow startled her from her scrutiny. She jerked her head up and peered at Violet over the microfiche machine. "Sorry, so I need to go?"

Violet pointed to a clock mounted on the wall behind the counter. "Fifteen more minutes."

Cheryl looked back at the microfiche screen. "Right. Sorry. I'll finish up."

Violet nodded, her rubber-soled shoes scuffing the wooden floor as she went to clean up the coffeepot and leftover cider.

Cheryl once again reached for the Off button on the microfiche, but hesitated before actually pushing it. Datschel Watters stared at her from the article. The Amish did not typically allow photos, which explained why there was no picture of Trampas, but this picture...

She frowned as she realized what she was looking at was very likely a police photo. The older Watters brother was handsome and clean-shaven. Unmarried? Most likely, since the Amish waited to grow their beards until after their wedding. And he was sad. Cheryl's heart grew heavy at the look of sorrow in the man's eyes.

She blew out a sigh and pushed the Off button on the microfiche. Whatever had happened between the two brothers was destined to remain a mystery. She had things she needed to research, but a decades-old death was not one of them.

A second later, Datschel Watters's face winked from sight.

Chapter Four

Despite her intentions, Cheryl found the mystery behind Trampas Watters's untimely death rarely left her thoughts. The Watters family had lived in Sugarcreek once. What happened to them? She had been coming to Sugarcreek since she was a little girl. Why had Aunt Mitzi never spoken of them? And what had become of Datschel?

Cheryl shook the image of his haunting eyes from her thoughts as she locked up the Swiss Miss and proceeded toward home. It was Wednesday night, and she had just enough time for a quick bite before heading to church for the midweek service.

Cars lined the parking lot by the time Cheryl arrived at church. Though it was only a quarter after six, it was already dark and the street lights cast circles of light around several people talking in huddled clusters. Rain had threatened all day, and there was a decided nip in the air, so rather than linger outside, Cheryl hurried toward the sanctuary where one of the church matriarchs, Mazee Stillwell, was leading a ladies' Bible study.

Cheryl enjoyed Mazee's style of teaching. She was patient and knowledgeable, but rather than trying to impress others with how much she knew, Mazee encouraged participation. When questions arose, she often sought the answers from members of the class, which Cheryl learned had deepened the relationships and trust the women of her church had for one another. This week's lesson centered on the Lord's sacrificial love for His church, a message that Cheryl found herself hungry to receive. Nearly an hour later, she leaned forward as Mazee closed the study with prayer, but it was after she opened her eyes that inspiration struck.

Why not ask Mazee for help with the town history project? She was widowed now, but both her family and her husband's were longstanding members of the community. Without a doubt, she had knowledge to impart, though Cheryl would have to be tactful about how she broached the subject. After all, no one liked to be reminded of their age.

Cheryl waited until almost everyone had cleared the sanctuary before weaving her way to the front where Mazee stood packing her things into a brightly colored, floral print bag.

"It was a wonderful lesson tonight, Mazee. Thank you so much for sharing it."

Mazee's gentle smiled widened. "I'm glad you enjoyed it, dear." She straightened and laid her hand lightly on Cheryl's arm. "How is business at the Swiss Miss?"

This was one of the things Cheryl appreciated about Mazee—she knew the members of her church and took an interest in each one.

"Business is very good, actually, especially now with the holidays approaching."

Mazee's silver head bobbed in appreciation. "Glad to hear it. Will you be traveling home for Thanksgiving?" She frowned as she slid her bag on to her shoulder. "Let's see...where did you tell me your parents live?"

Cheryl fell into step beside her as they made their way up the aisle. "Seattle, and no, I won't be going there this time. With business at the store picking up, I just don't think I'll be able to get away. Maybe over Christmas."

A twinkle lit Mazee's blue eyes. "Well, I hope you'll make time to see them. Family is important, you know."

Cheryl answered with her own smile. "They certainly are."

They had reached the front door, and Cheryl slowed to a stop. "Say, do you have a minute? There's something I'd like to talk to you about."

Mazee tipped her head and peered at Cheryl like an earnest little bird. "Of course, dear. I hope there's nothing wrong."

"No, no. It's nothing like that," Cheryl replied quickly. "Actually, I'd like your help. You see, Dwight and Suzy Foster asked me about helping out with a town history project, but since I really haven't lived here long, I'm kind of at a loss as to where I should start. I was hoping I might enlist a couple of people who know more about Sugarcreek's roots than I do."

Mazee's lips turned in a brief frown. "Yes, it is a little odd that they would ask you...you being new to Sugarcreek, I mean," she clarified with an apologetic pat.

"Well, I think it has more to do with my uncle Ralph," Cheryl said and then went on to explain his connection to the festival.

"Well that changes things." Mazee nodded. "Yes, I can see why the Fosters thought you would be a good choice."

"Except that I'm pretty sure I'm going to need some help collecting some of the town's history," Cheryl said. "Which is why I thought I might check with you to see if you're interested."

Pleasure lit Mazee's face from within. "Why, I would love to help, dear." She scratched her temple lightly. "In fact, I still have many of my parents' old photographs from when the town was first being built. Daddy was a collector," she explained.

Excitement flared in Cheryl's chest. "Why, that would be wonderful. Do you think I could take a look?"

"Of course. Come by any time..."

Mazee cut off midsentence, her gaze fixed to something over Cheryl's shoulder. Curious as to what had captured her attention, Cheryl turned to see. Muddy waited several feet away, deep chagrin marring his lined face.

He shuffled both booted feet and then turned a pleading glance toward Cheryl. "Sorry to interrupt."

"No problem, Muddy. Give me just a moment." She turned to Mazee. "Can I come by sometime after work?"

"That will be fine," Mazee said, her voice a smidge strained. She clutched the folds of her coat tightly to her chin and then bustled past Muddy, pausing only long enough to nod in his direction before making her way outside.

Cheryl strode the few steps to where Muddy waited. "What can I do for you?"

"I...well..." His gaze dropped to the carpet, and embarrassment darkened his features. "It's a little cold outside..."

"Your coat!" Cheryl grasped his arm. "Oh, Muddy, I'm so sorry. It's in my car. Would you like to follow me?"

At his nod, she whirled for the door and made a beeline for her blue Ford Focus. The wind had picked up since she had arrived, and more than once she saw Muddy rub his knuckles over his thin arms.

"Here you go," Cheryl said, pulling the coat she'd gotten from the clothing closet out of her trunk. "I meant to give it to you Sunday, but you must have left before I could find you."

Muddy clutched the coat in his gnarled fingers. Gratitude shone from his eyes, warming Cheryl through despite the brisk temperatures. "Thank you, Miss Cooper."

"Just Cheryl," she said, grasping his arm in a tight squeeze. "And you're very welcome."

His gaze fell to his shoes once more, and he shied from her touch in a way that reminded her surprisingly of Levi. "All right. Thanks again."

He slid into the coat then shuffled away, his long legs eating the distance across the parking lot before he disappeared around the corner.

Where was he going? Where would he sleep?

The next time she saw him, Cheryl determined to find out. Now that the weather was getting colder, she didn't like the idea of him braving the elements alone, although what she might do about it required more consideration than she'd given thus far.

Shaking her head, Cheryl climbed into her car and made the short drive home. First thing tomorrow, she'd contact Pastor Lory to see if he knew of any shelters nearby. After that, she'd see about getting the information to Muddy. What he did with it from there was entirely up to him.

Chapter Five

The bell above the door to the Swiss Miss jangled merrily, and then Naomi blew in accompanied by a gust of crisp November air. On her arm was a basket she used to haul her jars of home-made goodies. Cheryl finished checking out a customer and then hurried over to lift the lid for a peek inside.

"Hi, Naomi. I sure am glad to see you. Did you bring the apple butter I ordered?"

Naomi erupted in gentle laughter. "Ja, I have it, and a few other things besides."

Cheryl drew her hand back and grimaced. "Sorry about my manners. We've just had so many people asking, and things around here have been busy."

"No need to apologize." Smiling, Naomi withdrew a jar of her prized apple butter and set it on the counter. "I am grateful so many people like my canned goods."

"They sure do." Cheryl marked the jar with a name and set it aside. "That one is for Delores, the receptionist over at the police department. I promised I'd save her a jar."

One by one, she removed the rest of the jars from Naomi's basket and lined them up on the counter. "That's a good batch," she said appreciatively. "Should tide me over for a while…or until the next tour bus comes through."

Which wasn't for another hour. She laughed and gestured toward the back of the store and her office. "Got time for tea?"

Naomi rubbed her hands together briskly. "Tea sounds *wunderbar*. It was quite chilly riding in the buggy this afternoon. It will be time for our mittens soon."

Confident she could leave the remaining customers in Esther's capable hands, Cheryl led the way to the office, where she grabbed two mugs and filled them with water.

"So?" Naomi watched as Cheryl popped both mugs into the microwave. "How is the research coming?"

Cheryl punched the Start button and sighed. "Well, I have to admit, it's pretty slow going. I keep getting distracted by the things I read when I'm looking." She pulled her gaze from the carousel spinning the mugs round and round. "Say, you don't happen to remember an incident that happened between two Amish brothers named Watters, do you?"

Naomi frowned and sat down at the desk. "Watters? No, that name is not familiar. Why? What happened?"

"Apparently, one of them drowned."

The bell dinged on the microwave, and Cheryl carried both mugs and the box of tea bags to her desk. "It was a pretty big story, at least it seemed so in a town the size of Sugarcreek. There were several articles. One even made it sound like the older brother, Datschel Watters, had something to do with his brother's death."

A look of horror crossed Naomi's face. "That is terrible. And they were Amish?" Her eyebrows rose. "No, that story is not familiar. It must have happened long ago, before Seth and I married, or I surely would have remembered."

Cheryl snapped her fingers and then handed Naomi her mug. "That's right. I keep forgetting you moved here from Dalton. Well, it was a long shot anyway. Just thought I'd ask."

"Is this one of those things that has you so distracted?"

"That and . . ." She shrugged. She couldn't exactly tell her best friend that her mind had been consumed with thoughts of her stepson. "Well, mostly just that."

They laughed, and then Naomi plucked a tea bag from the box and dropped it into her cup. "I think I would have been distracted by reading such a thing as well. I will have to ask Seth if he remembers anything about it."

"Or I could show you," Cheryl offered. She set aside her spoon and leaned forward across the desk. "I'm going by the library this afternoon after the store closes. Would you like to come?"

Naomi sat up in her chair, her eyes gleaming with interest. "I have a couple of errands to run, but I am certain I can have them finished in time."

"Great. I'll meet you at the library."

They shared a conspiratorial grin, and then Cheryl took a sip from her tea. She could hardly wait until closing time.

Clouds had gathered and a light rain had begun to fall by the time Cheryl entered the library. She shook the water from her coat and hung it on a peg to dry before winding through the aisles in search of Naomi. She found her browsing through a checkered Betty Crocker cookbook that, judging by its tattered spine, had seen better days.

Catching sight of Cheryl, Naomi shoved the cookbook back on to the shelf. "There you are."

"Have you been waiting long?"

She chuckled wryly. "Not really. I was just so intrigued by the story you told me this afternoon, I could not wait for you to get here."

Cheryl had to laugh. The Amish valued patience, and her sweet friend normally exuded the trait despite her many responsibilities. "All right then, let's get started. Have you seen Violet or Pam?"

"Just Violet," Naomi said, adding a shake of her head. "But she was busy helping people, so I did not stop to chat."

"I won't bother her then. Besides, I already know what I'm looking for." She led Naomi toward the back of the library and the cabinets filled with microfilm. When she pulled out a drawer, Naomi studied the boxes of film inside with interest.

"What is all this?"

Cheryl selected a box and carried it to the table. "Haven't you ever seen a microfiche machine before?"

She furrowed her brow, perplexed, as Cheryl removed the microfiche and loaded it on to the microfilm reader. "I have heard of them, but I have never actually used one."

Once the film was ready, Cheryl pulled out a chair and indicated that Naomi should take the one next to her. She advanced the film rapidly until she found the right article. It wasn't as shocking as the first time she'd read it, but the picture of Datschel Watters still drew her gaze. Something about the man's eyes begged her attention and left her with a feeling of sorrow in the pit of her stomach.

"Well?" she asked when Naomi finished reading.

Naomi sat back in her chair, her face looking as bewildered as Cheryl felt. "It is a heartbreak what happened to them, for sure and for certain."

"None of it rings a bell?"

She shook her head. "But that is not surprising. If this man was never charged, speculating on his innocence would have been considered gossip. People would most likely have let the subject drop."

Cheryl frowned. "So what do you suppose happened to him?"

"The article does not say." She tapped the machine. "Were you able to find anything else about him?"

"I didn't look," she admitted with a wry laugh. "I felt kinda guilty getting sidetracked when I was supposed to be researching the town's history." She tilted her head and studied her friend curiously. "You, on the other hand, could look for me while I pick out a couple of books."

Naomi grimaced and eyed the machine doubtfully. "I do not know. I have never worked one of these...what did you call it? Micro-fish?"

"Microfiche," Cheryl clarified. She paused as she was struck by another thought. The Amish did not use computers, except in instances where it was allowed in conjunction with their business. She laid her hand atop the machine. "It's not really a computer, Naomi. A microfiche system is strictly a compact document storage and viewing system. In this case, it's old newspaper articles. Is that okay?"

She nodded hesitantly. "I suppose, if you can show me how to use it."

"It's easy," Cheryl assured. She spent a minute demonstrating how to advance and reverse the film then rose from the table. "All right, I'll leave you to it. Let me know if you find anything interesting." She pointed toward an aisle on her right. "Last time I was here, Violet told me the research books were over there. I'll come back and check on you in a little bit."

Already bent toward the microfiche, Naomi gave a distracted nod.

Cheryl smiled as she wound toward the research books. Obviously, her friend found the Watters brothers' story as interesting as she did, but for now she needed to focus on Sugarcreek and learning what she could of its history.

Nearly an hour later, Cheryl had a stack of promising books under her arm. She carried them to the counter and was surprised to discover no one there. Setting the books down, she leaned to peer through the office window. The light was on, but no one sat behind the desk. Where was Pam? Or Violet?

Voices drifted from the handful of patrons browsing the library aisles, but Pam's or Violet's voices were not among them. Perhaps they were busy with inventory or helping someone in the back.

She left the books on the counter and went to check on Naomi's progress. She sat where Cheryl had left her, only now her hand covered her mouth and she stared, eyes wide, at the microfiche.

Cheryl instinctively slowed. "Naomi? Is everything all right?"

Her hand lowered, and she pointed at the screen. "Oh, Cheryl, come see." She vacated her chair so she could sit.

"What is it? What did you find?"

"Look."

Naomi had scrolled much further back than Cheryl had on her previous visit. The date on the article was written nearly two months prior to the one she'd read and displayed pictures of the town beneath a startling headline.

Cheryl read the words out loud. "'Amish Man Accused of Murder?'"

"Keep going," Naomi urged, her fingers fluttering nervously at the screen.

The feeling of unease grew in Cheryl's belly as she scanned the article glowing from the screen. Much of the information was familiar, but some was given in greater detail than the first page she'd read. Along with the brothers' names, this article cited their ages and told a bit about their family.

"Trampas was only twenty years old," she whispered. "That's so sad."

Next to her, Naomi's *kapp* dipped as she nodded in agreement. "But look what it says next." Her finger shook as she pointed to a place on the screen. "There."

Cheryl leaned forward and squinted to see the words clearly. "'Though officers on the scene appeared perplexed by the explanation, Datschel Watters refused to comment further on his brother's drowning.

"'Sources close to the family said they witnessed numerous altercations which had often led to explosive displays of emotion, a spectacle which is relatively unknown in most Amish communities. When questioned about it, Datschel appeared quite distraught and was only saved from comment by the timely interruption of one Ralph Porter.'"

Cheryl widened her eyes. "That's Uncle Ralph!" The exclamation drew several interested looks. "That's Uncle Ralph," she repeated more quietly, "but the reporter made it sound like he was intentionally keeping Datschel from admitting something incriminating."

"That is not the worst of it. Keep reading."

Cheryl scanned the last few lines again and picked up where she'd left off. "'Porter has been known to side with the Amish on occasion. The most recent example took place last spring when he spoke out in support of their conscientious objection to the conflict in Vietnam, despite limited public outcry. When asked about his relationship to the Watters family, Porter replied,

"'Someone has to protect their rights.'" Porter was then heard advising Watters to remain silent until representation could arrive—a fact which some onlookers considered suspicious. Others were heard to remark that Porter may have been present before police officials arrived, raising questions regarding exactly how much information is yet to be confessed.'"

By this point, the knot in Cheryl's stomach had ballooned into something more like a fist. She sat back in the chair, her breathing heavy and her chest tight.

"They must have been close friends for your *onkel* to have been involved," Naomi offered gently. "Maybe your aunt Mitzi can shed some light on what happened."

"She's never mentioned the Watters family before," Cheryl said. "Neither did Uncle Ralph before he died, at least not that I can remember."

"It was not a pleasant topic, for sure and for certain."

Cheryl lifted her head. "You think maybe that's why they never said anything?"

She shrugged and spread her hands wide. "Could be. When will you speak to your aunt again?"

"Not for another week or more. She said they were heading into the mountains to deliver supplies so phone service would be scarce." She frowned. "I'm not sure I'll be able to wait that long to talk to her."

She printed out the article then grabbed the sheets of paper and stood. "I'm going to see if I can find Pam or Violet. Maybe they can help."

Naomi resumed her seat. "I will keep looking through articles to see if I can find any more mentions of your onkel."

"Thank you, Naomi," Cheryl said, already searching the library for one of the workers. Aware of conversations wafting from the front of the library, she made her way back to the counter and was pleased when she rounded the corner and caught a glimpse of Violet's white kapp. Unfortunately several people beat her in line, and she had to wait while they checked out.

When it was Cheryl's turn, Violet reached across the counter for the stack of books Cheryl had placed there earlier. "Good evening, Cheryl. I assume these belong to you?"

"Hi, Violet. Yes, those are mine. Listen, do you mind if I ask you a couple of questions first?"

Cheryl's words tumbled over and bumped into one another. Violet peered at her over the rim of her glasses.

"I'm sorry?"

"I was hoping you could answer a few questions. Not about the books." She laid the newspaper article on the counter and spun it so Violet could see. "It's about this."

Violet's gaze drifted down to the newspaper article and then over Cheryl's shoulder. "Well, we are quite busy at the moment..."

"I know," she said quickly, "and I really don't mean to be a bother, but it is very important."

Lines formed on Violet's brow as she adjusted her glasses. "I suppose I could take a quick peek. What is your question?"

Cheryl turned the paper a smidge so they could both read. "The article is about two brothers who used to live here in

Sugarcreek. Watters was their name. Apparently, my uncle Ralph knew them. Do you remember hearing anything about them?"

The more Cheryl spoke, the more agitated Violet became. She fidgeted with her dress, and her fingers twisted the strings of her prayer kapp.

"I am sorry, Cheryl, I do not think I can help you. Perhaps if you asked Pam . . ."

"Actually, I'm really just wondering if you might have any idea what their connection was to my uncle Ralph. He's mentioned here in the article, you see." She pointed to her uncle's name and then peered expectantly at Violet.

Someone behind Cheryl in line cleared their throat. Violet acknowledged them with a short wave. "What about your aunt Mitzi? Couldn't you ask her?"

"I could, but she won't be in touch for another week or more," Cheryl explained. She shifted and pressed her hands to the counter. "You were born in Sugarcreek, right? Do you remember anyone by the name of Watters?"

Once again a voice sounded from the back of the line. "Excuse me, could I just ask a quick question?"

Violet peered past Cheryl and lifted one finger. "I will be with you in just a moment, sir." Her gaze returned to Cheryl. "I am sorry. I cannot help you." She laid her hand firmly on the books stacked on the counter. "Will this be all for tonight?"

Taken aback by the abrupt change in her manner, Cheryl nodded numbly and took the books Violet handed to her.

"Um...thank you." She shifted the load of books to her hip. "Do you think maybe I could come by tomorrow when you have more time?"

"The library is open, but I do not work tomorrow. Perhaps Pam can help you."

Gesturing to the next person in line, she dismissed Cheryl with a cursory nod. She had no choice but to collect the rest of her things and leave.

Naomi bustled to her side, jamming her arms into the sleeves of her coat. "Well? What did she say?"

"Nothing," she said with a frown. "Less than nothing, actually. I sort of felt like she didn't want to talk to me."

Her brows rose. "Really? Why do you think that?"

"I don't know." Cheryl spared one last glance in Violet's direction. It was possible she was wrong. Her reaction to Violet's reluctance could be nothing more than an injured ego...but she didn't think so, not when Violet was working so hard to avoid her gaze. What did she know about the Watters family that she was unwilling to share? More importantly, what did she know about Uncle Ralph?

Biting the inside of her cheek, Cheryl followed as Naomi led the way to the exit. It wouldn't be enough to just wonder what Violet knew. Deep down, Cheryl sensed she would have to find out. Unfortunately, something inside also told her she might not like where the information would lead.

Chapter Six

T hat was a heavy sigh." Naomi's voice drifted over Cheryl's shoulder, a welcome sound after a busy morning at the Swiss Miss. "Is something troubling you?"

Cheryl slid one last jar of apple butter on to the shelf and turned to her friend. "Sorry, Naomi. I didn't see you come in."

"That is because you were too deep in thought to notice anything else." She wagged her finger at Cheryl. "I know you, my friend. You can be quite determined when you set your mind to something, and I do not think in this case it is the history project. Am I right?"

The thought of sharing her concerns with someone filled Cheryl with instant relief. She lifted her shoulder in a half shrug. "Got time for a cup of coffee?"

"Always." Naomi chuckled. "Let us go sit for a minute while the store is quiet. Esther can handle any customers who come in."

As if she heard her name, Esther looked up, and Naomi motioned to her from across the store. At her nod, Naomi pointed toward Cheryl's office and then followed while she led the way.

"So now, tell me what is wrong." She shut the door while Cheryl fetched two cups and poured the coffee. "Surely you are not concerned about what that reporter said about your onkel?"

"No, it's not that exactly."

"Is it the history project? Are you worried about gathering enough information?"

Cheryl shook her head and set Naomi's cup on the desk then dropped into her chair with a frown. "No, I don't think I'll have any trouble with that part. In fact, I'm planning to go back to the library later today."

"So? What is on your mind?" She settled into a chair opposite Cheryl's and took a sip of her coffee.

"It's Violet, or rather, the way she acted when I asked her about the Watters brothers. She was so evasive. Why do you suppose she didn't want to talk about them?"

"Are you sure she was trying to avoid your questions? She did seem a little busy."

"I suppose." Cheryl frowned and tapped the handle of her cup with her finger. "I could try talking to Violet again, I guess."

Naomi shrugged. "What about the other woman you told me about?"

"Pam?"

She tipped her head, thinking. "Ne, not at the library. The woman from your church."

"Mazee Stillwell." Cheryl pushed up in her chair. "She did offer to help. In fact, she told me she had a bunch of old photographs I could look through. I forgot all about it." She reached for the telephone and pressed it to her ear. "I'll call her right now."

A few minutes later, she replaced the handset and fixed a wide smile to her lips. "She's free tonight. She said I could stop by after I get off work."

"What about the library?"

She shrugged. "I can go by there anytime I suppose."

Naomi gave an approving nod. "Goot. Well, I am happy you have that settled. Perhaps this lady will be able to shed some light on what happened with your onkel, and then you can focus on the history project."

Cheryl laughed at the pointed look Naomi directed her way. Leave it to her sensible friend to keep her on track. She lifted her coffee cup and took a tentative sip. Though she wanted to ask about Levi, she'd yet to work up the courage. She lowered her gaze and adopted a casual tone. "Speaking of the history project, I haven't really had a chance to talk to Levi yet. Do you think he'll be free later today? I could stop by the farm after I leave Mazee's house."

"Ja, I am sure he will be free. He and Seth are not working such long hours now that the harvest is over. Perhaps you could come for dinner?"

Cheryl set her cup down carefully. "Dinner sounds wonderful, but I wouldn't want to impose."

"Having a friend we love join us in sharing a meal is never an imposition." Naomi gave her hand a gentle pat. "After we eat, I will show you how to make that pumpkin custard you like so much."

Warmth flooded Cheryl's heart. What would she do without her sweet friend? "I would love to learn. Thank you, Naomi."

She gathered her basket and stood. "We will see you tonight then, ja? Supper is at six." She gave a wave and then slipped out of the office, her plain skirt swishing softly.

Cheryl blew out a contented sigh. God had certainly blessed her since moving here and taking over the Swiss Miss. Not only did she have a job she loved, she'd made some real friends, people she could depend on—a fact that made her even more certain the decision she and Levi made had been the right one.

Tossing a glance at her watch, she stood and then carried the empty cups to the bathroom. She'd rinse them out later. Right now she needed to get back to her customers and the store if she wanted to finish up by closing time.

Fortunately, business was steady enough to make the hours go by quickly. It seemed like no time had passed before she locked up and made the brisk walk home to feed Beau, her Siamese cat, and pack up her car for the drive to Mazee's.

Mazee Stillwell lived in the oldest part of town, which Cheryl liked to call the Historic District. Houses here were landmarks, many as old as Sugarcreek itself. She slowed as she approached Cedarville Lane and soaked in the sight of the stately old homes dressed in their fall finery. Wheat wreaths, cornstalks, and pumpkins, even a few scarecrows kept watch as she passed.

Finally, she turned through a large wrought-iron gate that opened on to a bricked drive. At the end rose Stillwell Mansion, the ancestral home of countless Stillwells. Though her husband had passed, Mazee still kept up the mansion faithfully, thanks to a handful of servants and her husband's vast fortune.

Cheryl parked near the door then grabbed her portfolio jammed full of the information she'd already gathered and exited the car. The front door opened before she'd even reached the steps, however, and a pleasant-looking woman in a plain brown suit welcomed her inside.

"Good afternoon, Miss Cooper. Mrs. Stillwell is expecting you. May I take your coat?"

"Uh...yes." Cheryl managed to shrug out of one sleeve before being efficiently shed of her coat by the housekeeper. "Thank you, Miss...?"

"The name's Baxter, miss." She extended her hand toward the hall. "If you will follow me?"

Convicted by the woman's impossibly erect posture, Cheryl pulled her shoulders back before falling into step behind her. Mazee awaited them inside an elegantly appointed drawing room. Her heels echoed against the gleaming bamboo floors as she crossed to meet them, and light from an intricate chandelier cast golden highlights on her silver hair.

She extended both hands and clasped hers tightly. "Cheryl, so glad you could come."

"Mazee, your house...," Cheryl began, a tad nervously. Her gaze roamed over the heather-green damask wallpaper and settled on the fire roaring in the marble fireplace. "It's absolutely breathtaking."

A blush colored Mazee's cheeks, and suddenly Cheryl didn't see the wealthy widow. She saw the kind, generous woman from church who chaired the Christmas toy drive and led Bible study.

"The house is beautiful, but…it was more my husband's style than mine," Mazee said quietly. She motioned to a set of plush red chairs. "Shall we sit down?"

Once they were settled, Cheryl pulled the portfolio on to her lap and extracted a handful of photos she had copied from the microfiche. "This is what I have so far," she said, mentally fumbling for a way to broach the subject of the newspaper article on the Watters brothers. Mazee had graciously agreed to help with the history project, and the last thing Cheryl wanted was to impose on her time.

"My, you *have* been busy." She slid a photo off the top and shuffled it to the back. "Oh, this one." She flipped a photo of Sugarcreek taken in the early sixties for Cheryl to see. "I remember when this one was taken." She pointed to an old diner with the name painted on the window. "Recognize it? That's the building where Yoder's Corner is now."

"I see!" Cheryl leaned in closer and took the photo from Mazee. "Wow, that is really neat."

"And this is the Swiss Miss before it was a gifts and sundries shop."

Cheryl smiled. "That one I recognized. I made an extra copy for Aunt Mitzi. I think she'll like it." She took a deep breath. "Did you know the family who lived in that house?"

Mazee tipped her head to one side, thinking. "I did. I was young, ten or eleven, I guess, but I do remember meeting them once or twice."

"You know a lot of the families in Sugarcreek. Is it from church? Have you always been a Mennonite?"

She laughed, a pleasant sound that filled the large room. "I know most of them, I suppose. And no, I haven't always been Mennonite. I joined after my husband passed away. I needed something to take my mind off of my loss I suppose, and the church seemed like a good way to meet new people." Her glance returned to the photos. "Of course, the town was a lot smaller when these were taken. Back then everyone pretty much knew everyone else. Why, I can still remember when the old schoolhouse closed down and the new one went up in its place. It was a sad day for me. That old building held a lot of fond memories. In fact…"

She rose and crossed to a writing desk. On it sat a fat manila envelope. Mazee picked it up and carried it back to Cheryl.

"I thought you might find some things you could use in here."

"Wow, that's a lot of photos," Cheryl said, weighing the size of the envelope in both hands.

"My father was a bit of a historian," Mazee explained. "He collected old photographs, maps, letters, anything he could find, really."

She reached for the envelope and removed half of the contents. As she'd indicated, it was more than just old photos. Cheryl spied two old railroad maps right away.

"This will be great." She fingered the edge of one of the maps. "I'll take these to the church and have copies made of anything I think we can use though. I wouldn't want to risk something getting damaged."

Mazee shrugged and waved one hand dismissively. "Papa was the only person who really cared about that stuff. I'll just be happy if some of it gets put to use instead of staying jammed inside that old envelope."

Cheryl sifted through several old photographs, certain as she did so that she'd made the right decision asking Mazee to help. But the more she looked, the less inclined she became to talk to her about the Watters family. After all, she hadn't even asked Aunt Mitzi about it. Maybe she could clear up Uncle Ralph's part in the mystery. And it wouldn't smack of gossip.

Mazee placed her hand gently on Cheryl's elbow. "So what do you think, dear? Will you be able to use these old pictures?"

She looked up with a smile. "I'm sure I will. Thank you so much." She held up the envelope. "May I take these with me so I can sort through them at home before I make the copies?"

"Of course." Mazee clasped her hands together, and excitement sparkled in her gaze. "Oh, I can't wait to see you come up with for the history project. I just can't tell you how glad I am that someone has taken an interest."

"Me too. I really think it's going to be great once it's all finished."

Cheryl attempted to slide the pictures back into the envelope, but hard as she tried, she couldn't quite make them fit all the way in. "Well, sugar and grits."

"What's wrong, dear? Do you need some help?"

"I'm not sure." She turned the items one way and then the other. "I think there's something stuck down near the bottom of this envelope." She held the photographs toward Mazee. "Would you mind holding these for a second?"

"Of course."

Both craned to peer into the envelope as Cheryl shoved the flap back and pinched the sides to widen the opening. Sure enough, a crumpled photo lay mushed near the bottom. Cheryl reached inside and pulled it out.

"Ah, there was your problem," Mazee said, smiling as Cheryl smoothed out the photo. "Do you want to put that one on top?"

Cheryl said nothing, stunned as she was by the item in her hand.

"Cheryl?"

"S-sorry," she stammered.

Her gaze fluttered back to the photo. Staring up at her, his face rumpled and crisscrossed with lines where the paper had been folded, was Datschel Watters.

CHAPTER SEVEN

Y ou knew him?" Cheryl held up the photo of Datschel Watters, or more accurately, the newspaper clipping. She quickly realized that what at first had appeared to be a picture was indeed an article someone had snipped from an actual paper.

Mazee took the paper gently from Cheryl's fingers. "Oh my. I didn't even realize Papa had kept this." She blinked several times before lifting her gaze. "Yes, I knew the Watters family. Very sweet people. Amish, I believe."

Rather than returning the clipping to the envelope, she laid it atop the coffee table. "How do you know him?"

Excitement trickled through Cheryl, pushing her to the edge of her chair. "I ran across an article about him down at the library."

Mazee pressed her lips together firmly and shook her head. "Terrible shame, all of that. That poor family didn't stand a chance against that reporter...what was his name?"

"Jackson Mathers," Cheryl said, recalling it from the first time she'd read it in the byline.

"That was him." She gave another frown, this one more pronounced. "Never did care much for his style of writing. It was always so sensationalized. Nothing like what I thought was fitting for a small-town newspaper."

"So, then, what *did* happen?" Cheryl set the envelope aside and reached for the article. This was not the one that contained the mention of her uncle, but she could still get a clearer picture of his involvement from Mazee. "Do you remember any of the details at all?"

She cleared her throat. "Well, it was all so long ago. I've forgotten most of the story..."

"Of course," Cheryl said quickly. "It's just that some of the articles I read actually mentioned my uncle, so of course I was hoping to find out what I could about what happened."

If the announcement surprised her, Mazee didn't let it show. "Have you spoken to Mitzi?" she asked instead.

"I intend to, but she won't be within range of a telephone for another week or more. That's why I was hoping you might know something."

"I see. Well, that is unfortunate."

Cheryl tamped a tremor of excitement. "So how did you know Datschel?"

"We were the same age." Mazee folded her hands tightly in her lap. "I'm terribly sorry, Cheryl, but I'm not sure I understand what this has to do with the history project."

She shook her head, more than a little chagrined. "Nothing, really. I was just so fascinated by the story..."

"Fascinated?"

"Yes, well, it was unusual to see an Amish man arrested..."

"His brother drowned."

Cheryl hesitated at the note of disapproval she heard in Mazee's voice. "Yes, I read that in the article...," she began slowly.

Mazee glanced at a slender gold watch on her wrist. "Well, I am so glad you stopped by this evening, Cheryl. I hope some of the information I gave you proves helpful." She stood, her back rigid. "You will let me know what you hear from your aunt, won't you?"

"Um..." Cheryl rose and hugged the bulky envelope to her chest. "Yes, of course I will. Thanks again for your help."

"No trouble, dear. I will see you Sunday?" She moved to the door, inviting...no...*demanding* that Cheryl follow.

"Oh yes. I'm looking forward to it." She paused when she reached Mazee. "Listen, I didn't mean to upset you. I hope nothing I said..."

Mazee's shoulders relaxed slightly, and her lips turned down in a sad sort of smile. "It's nothing you said. It's just that Trampas's death was very hard on our little town, and being reminded of it so suddenly...well...the whole situation was difficult, really. A lot of people formed opinions one way or the other, and it caused division even among friends and at church"—she waved her hand—"pretty much everywhere. I hope you aren't planning on dredging any of that up after all these years. It was so painful for everyone involved."

"I..." Cheryl hesitated, restrained by the look of pleading she saw on Mazee's lined face. "No, I wasn't planning on dredging it up. I'm sorry I mentioned it."

Mazee gave a firm nod that declared the matter settled, at least in her mind. "Wonderful. Thank you, Cheryl." She walked her to the door where Ms. Baxter already waited with Cheryl's coat.

When Mazee turned, her smile was firmly in place. "Now, let me know if I can be of any more help...with the history project."

The slight pause made Cheryl think she clarified on purpose. She nodded. "I will. Thank you, Mazee."

"You're very welcome, dear. Good night."

"Good night."

What? Cheryl glanced at the bulging envelope in her hand. *What just happened?*

She walked slowly to her car, pondering their conversation and more curious than ever regarding the events surrounding Trampas's death, despite what she'd told Mazee. The man had drowned over forty years ago, and Mazee still feared talking about it would dredge up hurt feelings?

Her car bell dinged as she unlocked the door and climbed inside. She glanced at the clock on the dash. She'd spent less than half an hour with Mazee, which meant she wasn't in a hurry to get to the Millers' house before dinner. Maybe when she got there, Naomi could help her sort all of this out.

She sighed in frustration as she eased on to the road. Mazee had a valid point when she said she didn't want anyone dredging up old hurts, but Cheryl hadn't even had a chance to ask her about Uncle Ralph's part in the story.

Her conversation with Mazee swirled around in her head as she traveled the country roads and finally crossed the bridge leading to the Millers' house. Lantern light winked from the barn and other outbuildings, which meant Seth and his sons, Levi, Caleb, and Eli, were probably still hard at work. The chores were never-ending on a farm, Cheryl had learned, but it was a life she'd come to appreciate, even envy. The only strife here was the kind nature caused when the crops refused to flourish or the frost came too early. Nothing like what she'd known in Columbus or what she read about in the newspaper.

She gave a shake of her head as she put the car into Park and reached for her purse and the envelope stuffed with photos. She'd think about all of that again after supper. Right now she'd be content to share a good meal and maybe learn how to make a killer pumpkin custard.

The Millers' house smelled delicious and warm, just as an Amish house should. The inviting scent of baked bread tickled Cheryl's nose as she entered without knocking—an Amish custom she was only just beginning to feel comfortable doing. She took off her coat and hung it on a peg alongside several others before calling out.

"Anyone home?"

"Hello, Cheryl! We are back here," Naomi called.

She smiled as she entered the kitchen. "Hello, everyone. You all look busy."

A chorus of greetings followed. It didn't surprise her to find everyone in the kitchen. She'd learned long ago that this was the heart of the Miller home. Naomi and her daughters bustled about. By the look of things, dinner preparations were in full swing. Cheryl fastened an apron around her waist and joined Elizabeth at the counter where she was busily slicing a loaf of bread.

"Can I help?"

"Of course." Elizabeth smiled and handed her the knife.

"We are so glad you could come for supper," Naomi said from the stove. She gave the large pot one last stir then tapped the spoon against the side and laid it on the counter. "How did your visit with Mazee Stillwell go?"

Cheryl grimaced as she pushed the knife through the bread. "Not well, I'm afraid. I'll tell you all about it after dinner."

Several curious glances fluttered her way, but no one voiced their questions. Normal chatter resumed—everything from this week's canning to an upcoming singing that Esther hoped to attend with Lydia Troyer. Cheryl was glad to be a part of it and couldn't help but smile so wide it made her cheeks hurt.

A few minutes later the men came in, their heavy boots and boisterous voices adding to the noise clamoring through the kitchen. Naomi shooed them toward the washbasins then urged the girls to set the table.

She joined Cheryl near the counter while the others carried platters of food into the dining room. "Are you all right? You are quiet this evening."

Cheryl cast a glance over her shoulder at the rest of the Miller clan. "Just can't help thinking about family and how important they are," she whispered back. "I guess it's because Uncle Ralph has been in my thoughts so much the last couple of days. I miss him and Aunt Mitzi a lot."

Naomi gave her arm a gentle squeeze. "I miss them too." Her chin lifted, and she gestured toward the dining room. "Come. Let's enjoy our supper before the food gets cold."

Tucking her arm through Cheryl's, she led her toward a seat at the table next to the one Levi would soon fill. The last time she'd found herself seated next to him, it had felt warm, even natural. Would things be awkward now that they had voiced their feelings to one another?

"Hi," he said, smiling down at her as he took his place.

"Hi."

It was all they had time for before Seth invited everyone to take part in a silent prayer of thanksgiving. A reverent hush fell until almost at the same moment commotion erupted on every side. Cheryl had yet to figure out how they did it since no one actually said "amen." Perhaps they all simply took their cue from Seth, who lifted his head and reached for the cabbage casserole.

"I did not know you were coming tonight," Levi said, passing Cheryl a platter laden with roasted chicken. "It is a pleasant surprise," he added more quietly but still loud enough to be heard among the many voices.

When she glanced at him, his blue eyes held a smile, and Cheryl felt her cheeks warm with pleasure.

She matched his low tone. "How's the work in the barn coming? Have you finished putting everything away for winter?"

He nodded. The Millers always took very good care of the equipment used to run their farm, which included making sure everything was oiled and in good repair before being stored for the long winter months. In fact, because of the care they'd been shown, many of the tools Levi used had been handed down through several generations.

"Daed is thinking about adding a few beans to the crop next year." He scooped up a spoonful of peas and deposited them on his plate.

"Will he have space for that? I thought he had every square inch of land accounted for."

"He will if we purchase a few acres across from the petting zoo."

"He's thinking of buying more land?"

She took the bowl from Levi, surprised when he held on. Something in his gaze—an earnest sort of searching—made her breath catch.

"Not Daed." After what seemed an eternity, he broke the intense moment with an awkward smile. "I have been toying with the idea recently."

Cheryl cast a quick glance around the table and lowered her voice. "But what about your uncle Silas's land? I thought you were planning to move there…eventually."

She couldn't quite bring herself to say "when you get married." Apparently, neither could he.

"Uncle Silas's land will give me a good start, but I will need to increase that if I hope to provide for a family…you know…when the time comes."

He let go of the bowl, and thankfully Cheryl had enough of her wits about her to keep from spilling the peas in her lap.

"That"—she licked her lips and lowered her gaze—"sounds like a wise plan."

But if he really was thinking of the future, did that mean he could envision a life with her? Had God revealed the path Levi had said he would be praying for? And if it wasn't her he was thinking of making a life with, then...who?

Her heart cramped at the possibility of him planning a life with someone else. It wasn't as though she had any claim on him, in fact, the opposite. And there was the matter of their agreement not to act on their feelings to consider.

The scrape of forks against plates joined the chorus of sound echoing through the dining room. Cheryl took a bite of her mashed potatoes but couldn't enjoy their warm, buttery flavor for the thoughts swirling inside her head.

She and Levi had grown closer over the months, of that much she was certain. But she had accepted the fact that she could not ask him to leave his church, not when it meant so much to his family. Her gaze drifted to Seth and then Naomi. Naomi had told her of people who'd left the Amish church for the less exacting Mennonite. But would Levi even consider it?

She risked a sidewise glance and was surprised to see him watching her. In his eyes she saw reflected the same troubled uncertainty she felt.

"Cheryl? You have barely touched your food. Are you not hungry?"

Cheryl's head swiveled toward Naomi. "Oh...yes." She picked up her fork. "I was just..." She scooped up some peas and held them aloft. "These are delicious."

Naomi gave an uncertain smile, but thankfully conversation resumed full swing, and Cheryl finished the rest of her meal quietly. After supper she found it much easier to concentrate once

Levi excused himself with the other men and she was left alone with Naomi learning to make custard.

"You are preoccupied tonight," Naomi said, pouring a good amount of sugar directly from the container into a pot. "Is there something you would like to talk about?"

Cheryl sighed. At some point, she and Naomi would have to talk about her feelings for Levi, but not tonight. She reached for the envelope Mazee had given her and pulled out the photos.

"I suppose I'm just a little disappointed with the way things went this afternoon. I wasn't expecting Mazee to be so reluctant."

"Did she say why?" She sprinkled a bit of cinnamon into the pot and gave it a stir.

"Just that it was a difficult time for the town, and she didn't care to revisit it." Cheryl leaned over the stove to look at Naomi's handiwork. "I can never get over how you do that."

"Do what?" Naomi grabbed a saltshaker and poured a bit into her palm.

"That thing…cooking without measuring anything or using a recipe. How do you manage it?"

Naomi smiled and whisked a generous helping of half-and-half into the pot. "Experience. You do something over and over, and it becomes second nature. So what else did Mazee say?"

"Well, she admitted she knew the Watters family," Cheryl said. Propping both elbows on the counter, she skimmed through the contents of the envelope. Not finding the picture she sought, she went back to the beginning and riffled more slowly through each one.

Naomi slowed her stirring. "What are you looking for?"

"Oh…just…sugar and grits. It's got to be here somewhere." She split the pile in two and began laying the photos aside one by one.

Naomi set down her spoon and wiped both hands on her apron. "Did you lose something?"

"I didn't think so…but…"

Cheryl picked up the envelope and searched inside and underneath. There was no doubt about it. The photo of Datschel Watters was gone.

Chapter Eight

It's gone!" Cheryl threw the envelope on to the counter in stunned disbelief. "The picture of Datschel is missing."

Naomi frowned as she bent to pick through the photos. "Was it different from the one we saw at the library?"

"No," Cheryl admitted, "it was the same one, but it's still awfully strange. Why would Mazee keep it?"

"Are you certain she did?" Naomi pushed the stack of photos back toward Cheryl. "Perhaps you misplaced it or it fell out when you got out of the car. Should we check?"

She started to rise, but Cheryl motioned her to stay as a faint memory flashed into her brain. "Come to think of it, I may have left it with her on accident. We were talking about the brothers, and Mazee said she couldn't believe her father had even kept the article." She grabbed a short lock of hair at the nape of her neck and twisted it around her finger. "I was so preoccupied, maybe I left it sitting on the table and didn't even notice."

"Ach, so there you have it." Naomi smiled and went back to stirring her custard. "So what do you plan to do now that Mazee is unable to help?"

Cheryl sank into her seat with a sigh. "Go back to the library, I guess. It's either that or wait until I hear from Aunt Mitzi."

The spoon stopped its rhythmic scraping. At the stove Naomi stood staring into space, deep in thought.

Cheryl raised her eyebrows. "You have a better idea?"

Naomi tapped the spoon against the side of the pot and then set it on a plate. She turned to Cheryl, her hands braced lightly on her hips. "Actually, I was thinking...perhaps you could ask your onkel Ralph."

"What? Ask my..."

Naomi was aware of Uncle Ralph's passing, so her statement made no sense.

Seeing her confusion, Naomi lifted one hand and shook her head. "Ne, what I mean is, perhaps you could search through his things. Did not you tell me there were several boxes in the basement you had not looked through? Who knows? Maybe you will find something that will explain his involvement with the Watters brothers."

"You mean his photographs?" She sat up straighter. "Yes, I'm sure you're right. I did say there were a lot of boxes in the basement of Aunt Mitzi's house. I only looked through part of them when we found the photographs of Ruth's oars."

Speaking Ruth's name suddenly reminded Cheryl that she and Seth had been married in November, a fact which automatically made this time of year difficult for her friend. She grimaced in apology.

"Sorry, Naomi. I didn't think."

Naomi smiled and reached across the counter to pat Cheryl's hand. "Do not be sorry. I am not hurt simply because someone speaks Ruth's name, in this month or any other." She paused and scratched her temple. "I just thought of something else you might try... perhaps you might speak to the Vogel brothers."

"Rueben and Ben? Why?"

Naomi went back to the stove and, using a pot holder, poured the custard from the pot into a large bowl. She talked as she worked, the routine of making pumpkin custard so familiar, she completed the task without thought. "Well, they have lived in Sugarcreek for many years, and Ben would be approximately the same age as the younger Watters brother. Perhaps they remember something about them. They might even be able to tell you what happened to Datschel after the investigation ended."

Cheryl chewed her lip thoughtfully then gave a slow nod. "You're right. That's a very good idea. I'll talk to them the next time they come into the store." Her chair creaked as she shifted her weight. "And I suppose I could run into the police department and talk to Chief Twitchell. He wasn't working there at the time, of course, but there may still be records." She shrugged. "Wouldn't hurt to ask."

Naomi set the pot in the sink and then popped the custard into the gas-powered oven and braced both hands on her hips proudly. "There. We will have a fine custard shortly."

Cheryl took a long, deep whiff. "It smells wonderful already." She frowned. "Do you suppose I'll ever be able to cook anything as good for my..."

She broke off, embarrassed to realize she'd been about to say "for my husband."

"Ja. I do. You will make a fine wife and mother someday, for sure and for certain."

Naomi met her gaze squarely, her eyes brimming with a confidence Cheryl didn't quite feel and only sometimes believed.

"Thank you, Naomi." She pushed up from her chair. "Well, it's getting late. I suppose I'd better get going if I want to sort through Uncle Ralph's things."

Naomi paused from drying her hands on the apron at her waist to glance at Cheryl and then the oven. "But what about the custard? Are you not going to wait until it is done so you can try it?"

Cheryl patted her waistline with a wry grimace. "Much as I'd like to, these old jeans are fitting just a tad too snug. You'll let me know how it turned out?"

"I will," Naomi said. "And you will let me know if you find anything in your onkel's things?"

"Of course." She gave Naomi a firm hug. "Thank you so much for dinner."

"You are always welcome."

Cheryl pondered those words as she drove home. The Millers did always make her feel welcome. Almost like…family.

She pushed the thought away before it became too firmly fixed in her imagination. After all, she and Levi had already agreed they would remain friends. Unless God showed them another path, what good would it do entertaining impossible daydreams? And besides, she told herself firmly, right now the only family she needed to be concerned with was Uncle Ralph.

The bright red shutters on Aunt Mitzi's cottage beckoned as she turned off of Main Street and into the driveway. She smiled as she put the car in Park. Funny that she still thought of it as Aunt Mitzi's cottage, even though it had been home to her for over a year.

Inside, Beau greeted her with loud yowling the moment she opened the door. His protests turned to contented purring, however, when Cheryl set down her purse and the envelope from Mazee and scooped him up to hold him cradled in her arms.

Giving him a tickle under the chin, Cheryl turned him to peer into his crystal blue eyes. "I have a project for us this evening, old friend. You up to it?"

In response, Beau lightly nipped her finger and jumped to the floor with a thud. Tail twitching, he peered up at her as if to ask why she wasn't moving.

Cheryl laughed as she shed her coat and laid it over the back of the couch. Having a cat truly was like living with a grumpy friend. "All right, all right. Just let me grab a flashlight."

The basement of Aunt Mitzi's cottage was lighted, but Cheryl had discovered the last time she went digging around that a good flashlight came in handy when peering into and around the scores of boxes. She pulled one from the cupboard above the fridge, checked the battery strength, and then made for the stairs.

Cool air wafted up the moment she opened the door. Basements in this part of the state stayed perpetually cool since they were almost completely underground, and in the fall and winter, they turned downright chilly. She'd forgotten that while living in an apartment in Columbus. She fumbled for the light switch, found it, and flicked it on before starting down. At the top of the stairs, Beau sat watching her curiously.

Cheryl clicked on the flashlight and shined it back at him. "Well? Are you coming?"

His tail twitched, but he remained firmly planted where he sat.

"Some friend you are," she scoffed before making her way down the rest of the stairs.

Indeed, she would have welcomed his company, even if he was just a cat. Long shadows crowded the farthest corners of the basement where the glow of the overhead lights did not reach. She could easily let her imagination run wild down here, but to do so would mean scurrying back up the stairs with her mission unaccomplished. Armed with her flashlight, Cheryl picked her way through several boxes whose contents she already knew toward a stack near the back wall.

"Sugar and grits," Cheryl muttered, rubbing her arms against the dank chill. "Maybe I should have waited until morning to come down here."

No sooner had she finished saying it than a long, furry shadow caressed her ankles.

She squealed and leaped sideways, bumping a box of old clothes that split open on the floor with a bang, spilling the contents.

Cheryl eyed Beau crossly. "So you decided to join me?"

Her mischievous cat merely grinned—or she imagined he did based on the twitching of his whiskers—and leaped onto the stack of boxes she'd targeted to search.

"Fine, I'll let you stay, but you can't sit there." She shooed him on to a nearby stool and reached for the first box in the stack. Like many she had looked through before, this one was stuffed with old photos. Lifting the first few, she marveled at the skill and passion her uncle had displayed for photography—something else she hadn't known about until recently.

She closed the box, set it aside, and flipped open the flaps on the second one. More photos, but in this frosty environment...

She shivered. There was no reason she had to stay in the basement to sort through Uncle Ralph's things. She could always tote the boxes up a few at a time and label them properly when she was finished.

Her mind made up, she carried the first box up the steps, propped it into a corner of the kitchen, and then went back for the second. Both trips, Beau remained steadfastly at her heels. She had to admit, she appreciated his company, even if she did have to be wary of tripping on the stairs. Without him, it would have been far too easy to let her imagination create mysterious figures in the shadows, the way she'd done as a child.

She closed the door to the basement and then crossed to the thermostat and bumped it up a few degrees, hoping the added warmth would drive out the chill in her bones.

"C'mon, Beau. Let's grab a cup of tea before we get started."

She turned to reach for the teakettle, but her steadfast friend of a few moments before refused to move.

"What now?"

He eyed her quietly, his piercing blue stare mildly disconcerting.

"Are you coming?"

More staring, only now he crept toward her, his head lowered as though stalking, his eyes fixed to her forehead.

Cheryl's hand rose to her hair. "What? Do I have something...?"

Before she could finish, her fingers came away covered in cobwebs and something wriggly crawled into her collar. Giving a high-pitched shriek, she did a frantic, desperate dance to rid herself of the eight-legged menace. It hit the floor and then quickly disappeared under the cupboard.

"Spiders!"

She shuddered and bent at the waist to comb her fingers through her short hair, just in case her attacker had a friend. First thing tomorrow, she was fumigating the basement. Scratch that. Make it the entire house.

The boxes forgotten, Cheryl scampered straight for her bathroom and a hot *cleansing* shower.

The next morning, the boxes she had dragged from the basement accused Cheryl from the corner of the kitchen where she had placed them. She brewed herself a cup of coffee and then eyed them over the rim of her cup. She could sort through them this evening or...

She glanced at the clock on the microwave. She had less than an hour before it was time to open the Swiss Miss. More than likely, the Vogel brothers would be in for their game of checkers and she would be able to ask them about her uncle Ralph's relationship to the Watterses. After that, she hoped to make a quick visit to Chief Twitchell.

The boxes could wait.

Her mind made up, she carried her coffee to her bedroom to finish getting ready for work. A scant twenty minutes later, she hurried out the door and arrived at the Swiss Miss with just enough time to unlock the store, flip the sign, and boot up her computer before the first customers arrived. She kept one eye on the door as she bagged up their purchase but was not rewarded until much later when the bell above the door chimed and Rueben Vogel lumbered in. Cheryl scooched a box of leather goods under the counter with her foot and hurried forward to meet him.

"Good morning, Rueben."

"*Guder mariye*, Cheryl." He pulled out one of the chairs at the checkerboard and sat down heavily.

"Where is your brother?"

Rueben shrugged. "Late, as usual. Perhaps it is his age that makes him slower than molasses, ja?" He gave a playful wink but wiped his face clean of mirth when the doorbell chimed again and Ben Vogel stepped in.

"Guder mariye, *bruder*," Rueben called brightly.

He pushed out the chair opposite him with his toe and invited Ben to sit. Ben glanced at his watch and shot Rueben a critical glower before taking it.

"You are early."

"Am I? Must be my watch is fast. That, or my feet."

Cheryl couldn't help but smile. Now that healing had begun between the two brothers, she enjoyed their moments of brief banter.

Ben grimaced and reached for a checker, but Cheryl stopped him before he could place it on the board.

"Before you begin..."

Both men turned to look at her inquisitively.

"I wonder if I could ask you about something?"

Ben looked at Rueben, who shrugged.

"Of course," Ben said, laying aside the checker. "Our game can wait. What can we do for you?"

Cheryl took a moment to explain about the town history project and how her research for it had led her to the library. "While I was there," she continued, "I came across a very interesting article about two men named Datschel and Trampas Watters."

Their reaction to the names was very similar to the one given by Mazee. They peered at each other, and then Ben shook his head sadly. "Ja, I remember the Watters family."

He was the older of the two Vogels, so Cheryl wasn't surprised that it was he who responded. "And do you remember what happened to them?"

"Didn't one of them drown?" Rueben said.

"Yes, that was Trampas." Ben scratched his head, thinking. "It was summer, I think, about forty years ago or so."

Rueben leaned forward. "Trampas was the younger bruder?"

"That's correct," Cheryl said.

Ben looked at his brother and said something in Pennsylvania Dutch, after which, Rueben slowly nodded.

He lifted one gnarled finger to tap his temple. "Ach, I remember now. That was a long time ago, for sure and for certain."

Ben agreed and turned to Cheryl. "But I do not understand. What has this to do with your history project?"

The bell above the door rang, and a young man and attractive woman stepped in. Fortunately, they seemed content to browse, so Cheryl returned her attention to the Vogels.

"To be honest, what happened to Trampas is completely unrelated," she said, lowering her voice slightly. After all, it wouldn't do frightening the customers. "What I'd really like to know is if either of you can remember what part my uncle Ralph had in it."

Both men returned a confused frown.

Cheryl leaned closer. "I found an article that said something to the effect that he kept Datschel Watters from speaking to reporters until an attorney arrived. Why would he do that? Were they friends?"

Rueben pondered this a moment then cleared his throat. "Your onkel was well liked and respected by many in the Amish community. Many trusted him."

Cheryl nodded, aware that he was referring to the trust many Amish had shown by allowing Uncle Ralph to take pictures from afar.

"Perhaps it is not that they were close," Rueben continued, "but merely that the Watterses, like so many others, respected and trusted him."

"That could be it, I suppose." Cheryl frowned then gave a wave of her hand. "There is one other thing…the article mentioned disagreements the brothers had that apparently got rather heated. Do either of you remember that?"

Ben rubbed his chin thoughtfully. "*Hmm*…seems I do remember the two of them being at odds over something."

He thought a moment longer and then shook his head. "I am very sorry, Cheryl. I'm afraid my memory is not what it used to be." He looked at his brother. "Can you recall what it was about?"

Rueben shook his head. "I did not know them as well as you."

Her customers were slowly making their way to the cash register. Cheryl stifled a frustrated sigh. "Okay well, thanks anyway." She took one step toward the counter then paused and turned to look back. "If you think of anything, will you let me know?"

Both men nodded, but Cheryl could see they were already concentrating on their checker match. More than likely, they wouldn't give the Watterses another thought. And that meant whatever help she was going to get regarding her uncle's tie to them was not going to come from the Vogels.

CHAPTER NINE

Cheryl waited until Esther came into the store to relieve her for lunch before hurrying down to the Sugarcreek Police Department. Delores Delgado, the receptionist, greeted her with a cheery hello and a warm smile, only today something seemed missing. Cheryl stalled alongside Delores's desk, trying to pinpoint what it was.

"So?" Delores fiddled with her pencil, tapping the eraser against her blotter rapidly. "Don't keep me in suspense. What do you think?"

She reached up to push her dark hair behind her ears—ears that were not busy holding up a pair of thick black glasses.

Cheryl's mouth fell open. "Delores, are you wearing contacts? You look . . ."

"Dumb? Silly? Older?" She reached into her desk drawer and pulled out the familiar frames. "I brought them with me just in case I couldn't get used to the contacts." Her mouth drooped into a frown. "Maybe I should go to the bathroom and take them out?"

Her voice lifted at the end, as though she were uncertain and hoping for approval.

"I was going to say you look amazing." Seeing Delores's eyes brighten at the words, Cheryl smiled and shifted her purse higher on to her shoulder. "What made you decide to try contacts?"

A blush bloom on Delores's cheeks, and her gaze darted about the police station, though they were obviously the only two present. "Actually, I've been meaning to try them for some time. It's just... well you see, now... that is, have you...?" She reached for her pencil and resumed the rapid tapping. "What do you know about Brandon Richardson?"

Cheryl clutched her purse strap tightly. "The veterinarian?"

Delores's hand rose to her face in the familiar gesture she often used to push her glasses higher on her nose. She must have realized she wasn't wearing them because her hand fell back into her lap, and she nodded.

A knot the size of a baseball formed in Cheryl's throat. Though she and Brandon had never dated steadily, they had gone out a time or two. She had even felt a tiny prickle of a spark flash between them. It might easily have developed into something more had she not already lost her heart to Levi.

Suddenly aware that Delores was watching her with a slightly puzzled look on her face, Cheryl managed a tight smile.

"Brandon is nice," she said.

Actually, he was more than nice. He was a wonderful guy, and he deserved to have someone as sweet and pretty as Delores interested. Cheryl loosened her grip on her purse strap and stepped closer to the counter.

"He's really cute too. Do you like him? How did you two meet?"

Delores shrugged shyly. "I don't know him all that well, I guess. We met at a benefit he was hosting for one of the local humane societies." Her face brightened. "We're going out for dinner on Friday. I suppose I'll know him a little better after that, right?"

"Of course." She fumbled awkwardly for words. "If you don't mind me asking, whatever happened to that volunteer fireman you were seeing? What was his name?"

"Peter Dawes?"

"That's him."

Cheryl instantly regretted asking. Delores lowered her chin, and her expression turned sad.

"Things just didn't work out between us," she said, her shoulders slumping. "I don't think I was quite active enough for him. He was really into all those adrenaline rush kind of sports. You know, like mountain biking and cliff diving."

"I see." Cheryl fidgeted uncomfortably. "Obviously, that kind of thing isn't for everyone, right?"

"I guess. I did offer to try hang gliding with him," she continued, "except that I'm a little afraid of heights, so when we got to the airstrip, I had a panic attack and we ended up taking a walk by the river instead."

"Well, that sounds like fun," Cheryl said brightly.

Delores frowned. "Not really. It started to rain so we cut the date short and just went on home."

"Oh." What else could she say? Cheryl shrugged apologetically. "I'm really sorry, Delores."

She didn't answer, only lifted a corner of her mouth to chew on her bottom lip.

"Anyway, I'm sure you'll have a great time with Brandon. I'm happy for you, Delores."

She smiled shyly. "Thanks."

Cheryl gestured toward the back of the police station, relieved now that she could get on to the purpose behind her visit. "Is the chief in?"

"He is. Would you like me to ring him for you?"

"Would you?"

She nodded, but had to squint to read the numbers on the telephone keypad. Finally, she motioned for Cheryl to proceed. "He's ready for you."

"Thank you." Cheryl moved to the door but hesitated and looked back before going inside. "Hey, Delores?"

"Yeah?"

She looked up. In her hand, she still clutched the familiar black glasses. Cheryl pointed to them.

"If you like the contacts, great, but don't ditch the glasses because you're trying to impress Brandon. He's not that kind of guy. Okay? If anything, I bet he'll like you just because you're you."

Delores's smile lit her entire face. "Okay. Thanks, Cheryl."

"You're welcome."

That said, Cheryl turned and tapped lightly on Chief Twitchell's door. He invited her in, his voice a little less booming than normal. When she entered, he was running a tissue across an overly red nose and scowling.

"Miss Cooper, come in." He motioned to a chair that was set back from his desk a little farther than normal. "Have a seat, although you might not want to get too close. Confounded cold. Been fightin' it for over a week." He dropped the tissue into a wastebasket already overflowing with tissues.

"Thank you for seeing me, Chief. I'm sorry you're not feeling well."

He waved dismissively. "What can I do for you?"

Aware that he was in no mood for chitchat, she launched into the purpose behind her visit. She'd barely finished before he was shaking his head.

"Sorry, Cheryl. That case was before my time."

"I figured so," she said, easing forward to grip the arms of her chair. "Still, I figured I would stop by and ask, just on the off chance that you remembered something about it."

He leaned back in his chair, raising it on to two legs, his eyes lifted to the ceiling as he thought. "It was a long time ago, but I do remember hearing about it when I joined the force here."

"Really?"

He nodded. "There was talk after Andrew Bechnel resigned— you know, the usual gossip sort of stuff."

"You took his place as chief?" Cheryl asked.

He shook his head. "No, I was fresh out of the academy. Bobby Kramer was the chief after Bechnel. I took his place." He reached up to scratch his temple. "Anyway, the talk was that Bechnel resigned because he had feelings for an Amish woman."

"Violet."

He nodded. "Some guys wondered if maybe his feelings for her had mucked up his objectivity—made him unusually biased toward the Amish."

"Did you feel that way?"

He leaned forward and dropped the chair on to all fours. "I didn't know enough about the case to have much of an opinion on it one way or the other. Anyway, I'm afraid that's about all I can tell you. Don't rightly remember much more than that."

"What about the police records?" she asked, unwilling to give up and determined to track down every last scrap of information she could find. "Are any of those things still available?"

"Unfortunately, our records don't go back that far."

"Even on cold-case files?" she persisted.

He snorted, a sound that ended in a cough and with him reaching for more tissues. "You've been watching too much TV."

"You mean..."

"I mean the Watters's thing wasn't a 'cold case.' That's a phrase used to refer to unsolved crimes." He blew his nose loudly into the tissue and then crossed his arms and rested them on his belly. "Really, it wasn't even an investigation, not an official one anyway. Sure, police officers asked a few questions, but there was no evidence, nor sufficient motive, to pursue it any further. They determined it was an accident, pure and simple."

"That's what the paper said," Cheryl replied, disappointment seeping into her voice.

"So then, why come here? If you already knew it had been ruled an accident, I mean."

She shrugged and relayed the last bit of information involving her uncle. "With Aunt Mitzi out of touch, I suppose I was hoping you might be able to shed some light on the things the reporter said."

"Have you thought about askin' him?" Chief Twitchell sneezed then wiped his nose and tossed yet another tissue into the trash.

"The reporter?"

He nodded.

"I guess I could try to look him up," Cheryl said, rising when it appeared that the chief was on the verge of another hurricane-force blast. "Listen, I probably should go. And you"—she pointed to the chief—"should see a doctor."

He sagged weakly against the back of his chair. "Yeah. Maybe."

"Bye, Chief. Hope you feel better," Cheryl said as she reached the door. She grasped the knob and gave it a turn a split second before another sneeze sounded, this one loud enough to rattle the pencils atop the chief's desk.

Not a moment too soon, Cheryl thought as she waved toward Delores and left the station. She could almost feel the cold germs attacking. Any longer and she'd have been reaching for a tissue herself.

She glanced at her watch. The visit to the police station had only taken thirty minutes, which left her with half an hour for lunch. If she hurried, she could swoop into the Honey Bee Café and grab one of Kathy's famous Italian flatbread grilled cheese sandwiches to take with her before heading back to the Swiss Miss. Fifteen minutes later, she blew into the store, glad to see that while business was steady, Esther had things well in hand.

She set a classic cappuccino with plenty of whipped cream next to the cash register. It was one of Esther's favorites, and her eyes lit with pleasure upon spying it.

"Enjoy," Cheryl said, smiling. "I'm going to go into my office and wolf this down." She held up the bag with her grilled cheese.

"Take your time," Esther said, lifting the cup. "Thank you so much for this." She took a sip and breathed a happy sigh. "Delicious."

Oh, to be able to enjoy such a guilty pleasure without having to worry about the size of one's hips! Not that a grilled cheese was exactly on her diet plan, but Cheryl refused to feel guilty as she gobbled every melty bite. She'd have plenty of time to walk it off later . . . after she helped Esther manage the tour bus crowd.

Indeed, business did pick up substantially, and it was a while before she had another chance to even check the time. The clock on the wall above the counter read two minutes shy of three o'clock. Naomi had promised she would stop by the store early before picking up Esther for a chat, and Cheryl was impatient for her arrival. Not that she had much of anything to share.

She sighed. Ben Vogel said he remembered a disagreement between Datschel and Trampas, which was of very little help since he couldn't recall what it had been about, and Chief Twitchell had been even less helpful than that. At most, all he'd given her was a cold.

She sighed and walked into her office to finish up a few accounting chores before Naomi arrived. She pushed the power button on her computer and waited while it booted up. Once it finished, she decided to take the chief's advice and clicked on her search engine. She typed in Jackson Mathers's name. The reporter had been very prolific once. She found several articles he'd written—most for local news agencies—but nothing referencing the Watters's case.

She tapped her finger on the mouse, thinking.

"Knock, knock."

Cheryl had left the office door open a crack. Naomi poked her head inside and smiled.

"Anyone home?"

"Hello, my friend. Come on in." Cheryl stood and circled the desk, a smile ready on her lips. "I'm glad you're here."

Naomi's eyes lit hopefully. "You were able to speak to Ben and Rueben?"

"And the chief." Cheryl gave a frustrated nod. "Not that it did much good. The chief was no help, and the Vogels couldn't really remember much, other than the Watters brothers argued."

Naomi's shoulders drooped with disappointment. "And neither of them could tell you how your onkel was associated with them?"

"Unfortunately, no." Cheryl led Naomi back to the desk and turned the computer monitor in her direction. "Since speaking to the Vogels and Chief Twitchell were both a dead end, I thought I would see what I could find on the reporter who wrote the article, Jackson Mathers."

"And?" Naomi set her things down and eased into the chair next to Cheryl's. "Did you find something?"

"So far, I've only had a chance to look up some of his articles." She added the word *profile* to her keyword search and waited while the rainbow wheel spun. Finally, a couple of photos popped up, plus a single paragraph of biography that read very much like a resume, but nothing more compelling.

Naomi sat with her hands folded, watching Cheryl work. Finally she leaned forward and pointed to the screen. "I do not understand. Why are you looking for information about the reporter?"

"Well, Chief Twitchell suggested I speak to him." She waved her hand toward the monitor in exasperation. "I was *hoping* I'd be able to dig up some information on his whereabouts, possibly a phone number."

Cheryl turned off the computer with a sigh. "So much for that idea. It appears as though Mr. Mathers dropped off the grid after he stopped writing."

"The...grid?"

"You know...the Internet but more...like everywhere his information might be stored..."

"Oh. The grid. I see." Naomi grinned, and so did Cheryl.

"Yeah, it is a rather strange turn of phrase. Anyway, what it boils down to is that I'm not going to be able to call him to ask about what happened."

Naomi shrugged. "You could always visit the nursing home."

Cheryl froze and turned an incredulous stare on her friend. "You know where he lives?"

Her eyes widened. "Ja. I did not realize you did not." She gestured toward the computer. "You said you were looking for his phone number."

"Well, yes, but...never mind." Cheryl fluttered the thought away. "About this nursing home. Do you know where it is? What it's called? How far is it?"

Naomi tipped her head to one side, thinking. "I do not think I ever knew the name of the place. I just remember hearing that he had taken ill. He had to sell his family home—the one downtown next to the grocery store. That's when he moved into a nursing home."

"How long ago was that?"

She did a quick calculation on her fingers. "Five or six years ago, at least. Probably longer. The nursing home is in New Philadelphia somewhere. I could ask Seth, see if he remembers the name."

Cheryl shook her head. "I'll do a quick search. There can't be that many homes in New Philadelphia. It isn't that big."

Indeed, only eight locations popped up. The list would be longer if she expanded the search, but these at least gave her someplace to start. Cheryl placed a few phone calls and on the third try was told there was indeed a resident by the name of Jackson Mathers living at the New Day Retirement Village. She jotted the address on a sticky note then reached for her keys and handbag.

Naomi rose with her. "You are going now? But what about the store?"

Cheryl frowned and glanced at the clock on the wall above her desk. "You're right. I still have over an hour before closing. It's just...I was hoping to get over there before..."

She let the strap on her purse slip from her fingers. "Sugar and grits. I suppose it'll have to wait until tomorrow..."

"Ne." Naomi gathered up Cheryl's purse and placed it back in her arms. "Esther and I can close up the store. This is too important. Besides, I am curious to learn what your onkel Ralph knew about the Watters brothers."

She gave a playful wink and then shooed Cheryl toward the door. "Go on now, before it gets too late for you to stop by the farm on your way back and tell me what you have learned."

"Okay." Cheryl laughed and paused long enough to give her a quick hug. "Thank you, Naomi. I really don't know what I would do without you and your family."

She hesitated, realizing as she spoke the words how true they were and how much her love for the Millers had to do with her and Levi's decision not to act on their feelings.

Naomi made a "tsk" sound, but her eyes filled as she scuffed to the door. "A friend is like a rainbow, always there for you after the storm, ain't so?" Her voice gentled, and she patted Cheryl's arm as she passed. "Take care, my friend."

Cheryl gulped back a wave of rising emotion as she hurried out of the Swiss Miss toward home. Friends were important but so was family. Like Aunt Mitzi. And Uncle Ralph. She didn't know what had happened all those years ago between Datschel Watters and Uncle Ralph, but for her aunt's sake, she was determined to prove it wasn't a cover-up, as Jackson Mathers had implied.

At the cottage, she took a brief moment to check on Beau. As always, he greeted her warmly at first but watched reproachfully as she slipped back into her coat.

Cheryl set a fresh can of cat food on the floor next to his water dish. "I'm sorry, Beau. I promise I'll be home as soon as I can."

His blank stare never wavered.

"I know, I know. Tomorrow I'll stay home and snuggle with you all afternoon after church, okay?"

Still nothing.

Cheryl sighed and slid out the door. For now, she'd have to live with her cat's reproof. It was, after all, well-earned. With all the research she'd been doing after work, she hadn't spent much time with him the last few evenings.

She climbed into her car and then pulled the address of the nursing home from her purse and typed it into the navigation app on her phone. Almost twenty minutes later, Beau's feelings were forgotten as she reached the outskirts of New Philadelphia and steered the final few turns toward the New Day Retirement Village.

A wide stone gate greeted her as she entered the village. She had expected a traditional sort of "home" and instead found a series of small cottages, all similar in style and with a quaint appeal enhanced by a myriad of colorful mums, cornstalks, and various other decorations for fall.

She passed several manicured lawns, still pristine thanks to the lack of snow, and a row of pretty picket fences before finding the house she sought. She checked the address again.

"Sixty-four Apple Drive. This is it."

She turned into the driveway and put the car in Park. Unlike the other cottages she'd passed, this one was devoid of decoration. No pretty pumpkins dotted the sidewalk, and the porch lights did not beam in welcome, but through one of the windows, the glow of a television flickered.

"Someone's home," she muttered as she exited the car.

She took a breath and prepared to approach the house then at the last second decided she might do better if she had Mr. Mathers's articles with her and reached into the backseat to retrieve them. Sucking in sharply, she strode up to the door and rang the bell.

She didn't have to wait long. The light flicked on, the door swung open, and a slight man with stooped shoulders and graying hair eyed her over a pair of tortoiseshell glasses.

Snowy flakes dotted his shoulders, which Cheryl did her best to ignore. "Jackson Mathers?"

The furrows on his brow deepened. "That's me."

She licked her dry lips and stuck out her hand. "My name is Cheryl Cooper."

His grip was still strong, despite the wrinkles and age spots that dotted the back of his hand. "Pleased to meet you, Miss Cooper. What can I do for you?"

He released her hand, and Cheryl held up one of the articles. "I'd like to talk to you about this, if you have a minute."

His gaze switched to the article. After a lengthy pause, he frowned. "That was a long time ago." His gaze narrowed. "You Amish?"

She lowered the paper. "Do I look Amish?"

He studied her up and down and then shifted to lean against the door frame. "Guess not. Who'd you say you were again?"

"My name is Cheryl Cooper." She replaced the article and the others in a pocket of her purse, all the while fighting a feeling of guilty discomfort. Of course he wouldn't recognize her name, but he would Uncle Ralph's. She swallowed and lifted her head to meet his gaze. "Ralph Porter was my uncle."

"Who?"

She blinked, taken aback by his apparent confusion. "Ralph Porter? You mentioned him in your article."

She waved weakly at her purse. Could it be he'd forgotten? He was in a nursing home after all, or rather, an assisted living village. Maybe his memory was unreliable, or his health was declining and it affected his ability to recall facts...

"Porter. Right."

He spun and disappeared inside the house, but he left the door ajar, so Cheryl went in after him. His place was sparse but tidy, except for the enormous amount of mail piled on a sturdy console table. A moment later, he poked his head into the hall and stared at her.

"You comin'?"

"Coming. Yes. Sorry." She pressed her purse to her side and joined him in a makeshift kitchen—makeshift because she'd seen campgrounds better equipped. There was a mini fridge, the kind used in dorm rooms, and a row of compact cupboards but nothing atop them and no curtains hung at the window above the sink.

Mr. Mathers stood at a tiny stove stirring a pot that contained something that smelled like canned chili.

He tapped the spoon on the side of the pot then eyed her over his thin shoulder. "You hungry?"

She shook her head. "I ate before I came."

Which was partly true. She had eaten…at lunch. But she didn't trust whatever he had simmering in that pot.

He grunted and ambled toward a table outfitted with two chairs. He took one and gestured toward the other. "Have a seat, Miss Cooper."

She obliged but then wished she hadn't when she realized she'd have to sit sideways in order to keep their knees from bumping under the tiny table.

She twisted as far as the table leg would allow. "First, I'd like to thank you for speaking with me today."

He folded his hands on the tabletop, his knobby knuckles pushing against his wrinkled skin. They were reddened and swollen, as though he suffered from rheumatoid arthritis, a condition that had to have been painful for a writer, and she felt a flash of compassion.

She cleared her throat and tried again. "I came across your article during some research I was conducting on the town's history. I was curious about some of the details and wondered if you wouldn't mind chatting about what happened."

His eyes narrowed as he peered at her through the thick glasses. "That was over forty years ago, miss."

"I realize that," Cheryl said, encouraged that she'd at least gotten him to break his silence. "But it was such an interesting story."

She held her breath while she gauged his reaction. Mr. Mathers leaned forward, his blue eyes suddenly piercing.

"You say you're Ralph Porter's niece?"

She nodded.

"Heard he died some years ago. That true?"

"It is." She fought a sudden swell of irritation at the callous way he'd inquired about her uncle's passing—without gentleness or any expression of regret.

Mr. Mathers sat back against his chair with something akin to a smirk on his wrinkled lips. "Well then, Miss Cooper, I gotta wonder at your coming. After all, anything I tell you about what happened would tend toward my word alone...seeing as how you wouldn't be able to ask your uncle. You thought of that?"

Countless thoughts flashed through Cheryl's brain. Why should he suddenly look so smug? What could he possibly tell her that would require confirmation from Uncle Ralph? More importantly, what secrets had Uncle Ralph carried with him to his grave?

She formed her response carefully. "There aren't many people who remember much of what happened. Those who do aren't all that inclined to talk about it."

His eyes gleamed. "You been asking around, have you?"

"A bit."

Her chin rose under his careful study, but she held her tongue. He was a reporter, or had been when he was younger. More than likely his ego would prompt him to open up if she waited long enough.

His grin faded, and he nodded. Leaning forward, he planted his elbow on the table and jabbed his index finger in her direction. "All right then, Miss Cooper. I'll tell you what happened. But, missy, I can't guarantee you're going to like it."

CHAPTER TEN

There was something threatening in Jackson Mathers's tone—a note of foreboding that sent icy fingers wriggling down Cheryl's spine and made her regret coming to see him at all. Gathering the remnants of her tattered courage, she nodded for him to continue.

"It all started the night the younger brother drowned."

Cheryl felt a moment of helplessness as he drew a wheezing breath and reached up to tug at the collar of his gray flannel shirt. When he'd caught his breath, he said, "Although, I figure it really went back much further than anyone really knew."

He speared Cheryl with a steely blue glare. "They were competitive, those boys, even being Amish. A rivalry festered between them only a few people even guessed at. Everyone else in that two-bit town was too blinded by the plain clothes and religious talk to see what was really going on."

"You being one of the few who *weren't* blinded?" Cheryl said, though she suspected she knew the answer.

"You got it." He motioned toward the floor and her purse, where a corner of the article she'd shown him peeked out from a pocket. "The younger brother, Trampas…he entered several swim meets while he was on his running-around time. What do they call it?"

"*Rumspringa*," Cheryl supplied.

He gave a slow nod. "That's it. Anyway, I covered a couple of those meets as sort of a human interest story. Always was a lot of curiosity about the Amish, so when this boy started entering meets and winning, well, people wanted to know, and my editor wanted to sell newspapers."

Cheryl leaned forward, careful to avoid contact with his knee, but too interested to remain still. "He was good?"

He shook his head. "More than good. That boy had talent. I remember watching him and thinking he had to be part fish. The way he moved through the water, well, it was something to see."

His snort of disgust was unusually loud in the small kitchen. Cheryl jumped and then had to apologize when her elbow bumped the table, upsetting a silver saltshaker.

"Sorry," she said. She motioned for him to continue. "You were saying?"

He appeared confused for a moment. His frown returned, and he peered at her through narrowed eyelids. "His swimming—I was saying I couldn't believe all that ability got poured into one Amish kid who couldn't do a thing with it. What for?"

He rose cumbersomely and shuffled to one of the cupboards, grasping at the countertop for support. After a good amount of digging in one of the drawers, he pulled out a fat photo album and carried it back to the table. "I did several articles on him, actually, and was getting quite a bit of positive feedback…until a man came by one day and asked me to stop."

He dropped heavily into his chair then quirked one eyebrow and stared at her, waiting.

The reporter gave new meaning to the phrase "bated breath." Cheryl lifted her chin defiantly. "I take it you mean my uncle? He must have had a reason," she added without waiting for an answer.

"Oh, that he did, missy. That he did."

His voice had begun to rasp. He plucked a napkin from a holder on the table, coughed into it, and then wadded it into a ball in his palm. "He said the boy's father was upset by all the press coverage. Claimed it was causing division in the family and insisted I quit writing the stories."

Cheryl's nerves had caused a quivering in her limbs. Wary of Jackson Mathers's reporter's instincts, she clasped her hands tightly in her lap, thankful for the concealment provided by the skinny wooden table. "Did he say what kind of division?"

"Not at the time. I didn't know what he meant until later. Much later."

"After Trampas drowned," she whispered.

His lips stretched in a predatory sort of smile that reminded Cheryl of a wolf. She barely suppressed a shudder. The man had to be approaching his mid to late seventies, but he was intimidating nonetheless. She shivered thinking what he must have been like when Uncle Ralph knew him.

He gave a low, frustrated growl and smacked the heel of his hand against the tabletop. "I sensed something wasn't right about the story that other boy gave to the police. It was too cut-and-dried. Too perfect. Like somebody had coached him on exactly what to say. I figured there had to be more, but I never was able to get it out of him."

"It could have been the truth," Cheryl stammered. "I mean...the reason it sounded so cut-and-dried could have been because he was telling the truth. Did you think of that?"

He smiled cynically. "If you say so. No, I still think..."

"If you wouldn't mind?" Cheryl lifted one hand to stop him. "What exactly *did* Datschel tell the police? I couldn't find it in the article I read at the library."

Mr. Mathers slid the photo album toward her and motioned for her to open it. "It's near the middle there. An article I wrote just after the news broke that the boy had drowned."

Cheryl lifted one of the newspaper clippings from the album and held it aloft. Mr. Mathers shook his head and waved his fingers for her to continue looking.

"That's it." He slapped his hand down on to the next open page and pointed to the headline: Olympic Dreams Die with Drowning Victim.

His blue eyes gleamed as Cheryl looked from him to the headline. "You didn't see that one in the library, did you?"

She shook her head.

"I didn't think so. By that point, only one of the local papers was still printing my stuff." His tone had taken an accusatory note, as if he held her and everyone else in Sugarcreek responsible. "I blame the police department for the shabby way the investigation was handled. They were a 'good ole boy' system back then—hardly equipped to manage a murder investigation, especially one involving those Amish. They still can't, if you ask me. The new guy... that Twitchell... he isn't all that much better than the buffoon he replaced."

Cheryl's feelings regarding Chief Twitchell aside, she didn't like the way he referred to him or "those Amish."

"What exactly do you mean by 'good ole boy'?" she asked, careful not to let her anger show.

He gave a disgusted snort. "I mean everybody knew everybody. They were either related, or they went to school together, or..." He paused, and his lips made a slight sucking sound. "Or they were dating someone."

He pushed on before she could ask whom he meant. "That Datschel boy insisted his brother's drowning was an accident. Said they'd gone down to the river to talk and ended up in the water just to cool off. Except it was cold for that time of year, and dark. Datschel didn't even notice when his brother went under. By the time he got around to pulling his body out of the river, it was too late. That don't seem odd to you?"

He rapped the table with his knuckles and then pointed to his face. "The older boy had a black eye. Did you know that? He claimed he got it when he hit a log diving into the water to look for his brother. Convenient, eh? I told the detectives it was suspicious, but they were too ignorant to believe an Amish boy would lie to save his own skin. They took him at his word and didn't get around to questioning him until after his bruises healed. By that time, your uncle had just about everyone in Sugarcreek convinced that Datschel had done all he could to save his brother. I knew better."

Cheryl licked her lips, but ended up only adding to their dryness. "M-my *uncle* had them convinced? Why would he do that, unless he..."

He cut her off before she could finish. "Porter was a friend of the family. Took a lot of photos. I even used a couple for stories I was doing before all of this broke loose." He tapped the photo album with his index finger. "You're welcome to look if you like. I always gave credit where it was due."

She pulled the photo album close. "I'll do that. Thank you." She lifted out one of the articles that clearly showed Uncle Ralph's name below the photo and held it up by the corner. "Would you mind if I borrowed this? I'd like to take it by my church, Friendship Mennonite, and have some copies made."

He waved dismissively. "Keep it. I've got plenty."

Cheryl thanked him and slid the article into her purse with the others. She mulled over her next question and framed her words carefully. "About Datschel...you said Uncle Ralph convinced everyone of his innocence, but you knew better. What do you mean?"

His eyes took on an angry gleam. He shoved back his chair and rose to pace. His steps were slow and unsteady, but there was anger to the way his shoes smacked the floor. "Those Amish act all peace-loving, but they aren't any better than anyone else. They can be ruthless, you know. And stubborn. The boys' father didn't like all the attention his son was getting. Called it prideful.

Refused to go to the meets to watch his son swim. What kind of father does that?"

He said it with more sarcasm than Cheryl could swallow, but somehow she sensed he wasn't talking to her. He was rehashing the details of what had happened more than forty years ago in his head. She remained silent.

"But that Ralph Porter couldn't see it. Couldn't see what was right in front of his face. Took up for them, and...Oh, I see." His gaze shot back to Cheryl. He lumbered back to his chair and sat, his arms crossed. "You inherited a bit of your uncle's bias, is that it? You're close to those Amish too?"

She crossed her arms defensively. "They're good people, Mr. Mathers."

"Right. So good they'd cover up a man's murder?"

Heat rose in Cheryl's cheeks. "If that was what happened, I'm sure the police would have exposed it."

"Unless the chief had a friend who was close to the family. Someone he'd played ball with and trusted. Someone who encouraged him not to investigate."

She snapped her mouth closed and glared. How dare he imply that Uncle Ralph had done something so insidious?

Mr. Mathers grinned. "I told you, Miss Cooper. The only people who like the good-ol'-boy system are the ones who are in it."

"All right," Cheryl said, conceding his point, "so besides my uncle and the chief, who else was in this system?"

His eyebrows rose.

Cheryl shrugged. "C'mon. You say my uncle wanted this covered up. Who else was involved? And why? Was it only to protect Datschel?"

"There were a lot of people who wanted to protect him, yes."

"Like who? His family? Of course his father wanted to protect him, especially if he thought he was innocent."

For the first time, Mr. Mathers seemed uncertain. "Well...not just his father..."

Cheryl leaned in intently. If this man believed Uncle Ralph had helped cover up a murder, she wanted to know why. "Who, Mr. Mathers? Who else helped convince the chief to stop his investigation?"

"If you must know, it was his sister!" Clarity returned to his eyes, and he turned a pointed glare at Cheryl. "The chief had a thing for her and wound up joining the Amish so he could marry her." Seeing the shock on her face, the grin returned to his lips. "Now that's something you weren't expecting, was it?"

"Do...do you remember his name?" she asked meekly.

"Bechnel," he said curtly. "Andrew, I think."

Cheryl's heart lurched. "The sister's name wasn't by chance Violet, was it?"

Her question lassoed his attention. His sharp gaze zeroed in on her face. "Yeah, that's it. I'd forgotten until I heard you say it, but now that I think on it, I do remember her name being some kind of flower."

Cheryl sagged against the back of her chair. Violet used to be a Watters.

Which of course explained her harried reaction when Cheryl requested her assistance at the library. She'd refused to help not because she was busy...but because she was Datschel Watters's sister.

CHAPTER ELEVEN

Violet Bechnel. Violet Watters.

Cheryl pondered this new revelation all the way home. Jackson Mathers had said her uncle Ralph used to be a friend of the family. Why then had Violet refused to say anything? What mysterious details had kept her from telling Cheryl what she knew?

Deep down, she feared the answer.

Uncle Ralph had been as much a part of her childhood as her aunt Mitzi. Her summers in Sugarcreek, the festivals, the fun—she didn't have a single memory of those days that didn't have both of them in it. In fact, she always remembered them together, like a matched set of china—he the saucer that supported the more delicate and extravagant cup.

Sorrow soaked her heart. What would Aunt Mitzi think of Jackson Mathers's claims? Or did she already know? Cheryl tightened her grip on the steering wheel. Why did Aunt Mitzi have to be out of touch now, when she needed to talk to her so badly? A phone call would be useless. Aunt Mitzi had warned her there would be no service where they were going, but just possibly...

She arrived home and hurried to the mailbox, hoping she'd find a much-longed-for letter hiding there but was disappointed to see only a couple of circulars and a generic credit card offer. She trudged up the walk, junk mail in hand. Inside the house, Beau greeted her with a loud yowl.

Cheryl tossed the junk mail aside and scooped him off the floor. "What do you think, Beau? Any chance we have a message from Aunt Mitzi on the computer?"

He blinked and let out a soft mew.

"I don't think so either," she said, burying her face into his fur. Still, she couldn't help checking and was more than mildly disappointed when her inbox remained empty. After a moment, she sighed and carried Beau into the kitchen for a treat.

It wasn't late, but the sun had long since set, so Cheryl was surprised when a soft knock sounded on her back door. She cast a cautious glance through the window and spying Naomi and Levi, let out a pleased gasp and hurried to let them in.

"Levi, Naomi! Come in. I wasn't expecting to see you this evening."

The two bustled inside, and Cheryl closed the door on a crisp gust of winter air.

"Thank you, Cheryl," Levi said.

"We are sorry to drop by unexpectedly," Naomi added.

"Nonsense." Cheryl smiled and reached to take Levi's coat and Naomi's cloak. "This is a wonderful surprise."

Almost as though he wished to share his agreement, Beau scampered to Levi and rubbed against his pant leg until he bent to pick him up.

Cheryl smiled, watching. "Looks like he's glad to see you too. Both of you, I mean."

Realizing how much she'd revealed with the innocent remark, she spun to hang their garments on a row of hooks. When she was sure no trace of embarrassment lingered on her face, she led them to the table.

"What are you two doing out and about?" She cast a quick glance at Naomi. "Was everything all right at the store? I probably should have checked with you when I left Jackson Mathers's place."

"You found him then?" Naomi's head bobbed. "Goot. I hoped you would get to speak with him."

A smile twitched on Cheryl's lips. "So you came by to see what I learned?"

Levi shrugged and spread his hands wide. "I tried to convince her to wait until morning, but you know my maam. She can be very determined."

"And her hearing is also perfectly fine," Naomi chided but with a teasing wink. She turned her gaze to Cheryl. "So? How did your visit go? Did the reporter remember your onkel?"

"He did." Cheryl frowned. "But he wasn't very pleasant. Mr. Mathers made some pretty strong allegations about the Watters family"—she clasped her hands tightly as she bit back a flash of temper—"and Uncle Ralph."

She shook her head and then motioned toward the counter. "Can you stay for a bit? I'll make a pot of coffee."

Both Levi and Naomi nodded, so she put a pot on to brew while Naomi filled her in on business at the store after she left. Soon the aroma of fresh coffee filled her kitchen. She pulled three mugs from the cupboard, carried them to the table, and then returned with the cream and sugar for Naomi. Levi preferred his black.

She liked that she knew that fact, but couldn't look at him when she set his cup down.

"*Danki.*"

His sincere thanks for such a simple act warmed her through. His fingers curled around the handle of the cup and then their gazes met for a brief moment before she turned to give Naomi her cup.

"Danki, Cheryl." Naomi fidgeted with impatience. "Now, tell us about your trip. What did Jackson Mathers tell you?"

Cheryl cupped her hands around her mug and then drawing in a deep breath, shared the details of her visit. "The most shocking thing I learned," she said when she'd finished recounting what he'd told her, "was that Violet Bechnel used to be a Watters. Did either of you know that?"

"I had no idea." Naomi had been running her fingers down the strings of her kapp, but she stopped at this and turned to Levi, her eyebrows arched in question. "Did you know this, Son?"

He rubbed his fingers over his chin, thinking. "This is not familiar. Perhaps Daed would remember?"

Naomi nodded and looked at Cheryl. "Why do you suppose she did not say anything when we were at the library?"

"My question exactly." She tapped her index finger against the side of her cup. "Do you think she would talk to us, if we went to see her, I mean?"

"And what would you say?" Levi asked.

"Well, I suppose I would ask what she knows about Uncle Ralph's involvement in her brother's case," Cheryl replied. "And what she can tell us about Jackson Mathers's claims of a cover-up."

"Is that wise?" He frowned and tipped his head uncertainly. "If she did not want to talk at the library, why would she change her mind if you went to see her now?"

"Perhaps it would be different if we were not in a public place," Naomi suggested, her expression hopeful. She set aside her mug, her coffee untouched. "Also, if she knew we were only interested in protecting Ralph, perhaps she would be more inclined to help. He was, after all, a friend of the family at one time, ain't so? She must have known this and so would feel obligated to at least speak with Cheryl."

She looked to Levi. "But I do think it would be better if she did not go alone. You will bring us to speak to the Bechnels tomorrow?"

He agreed with a shrug. "Ja, Maam. I will bring you, if it is all right with Cheryl."

Though it shouldn't have, her heart fluttered at the thought of having him along all day. Fighting a suddenly dry mouth, she nodded and managed a shaky, "I don't mind at all."

"Goot. Then Maam and I will pick you up after church."

Cheryl quickly gave her consent.

Levi stood and went to fetch their coats. Before sliding into his, he draped Naomi's cloak gently over her shoulders. He was a strong, capable man, yet when it came to his stepmother, he displayed tenderness and caring. Cheryl couldn't help but be affected by it. How many times had Naomi stressed the importance of family? Of standing by one another and supporting each other. It was no wonder Levi was so concerned about her and Seth that he would set aside his own feelings…and hers…to keep from hurting them.

Cheryl shook the thought away. She understood Levi's motives and agreed with them. Standing by one's family *was* important. She wanted to do the same for Uncle Ralph. His reputation meant a lot to her, even though he was gone. She blinked against a sudden swell of tears and walked with them to the door.

At the threshold, Naomi stopped and wrapped her in a tight hug. "We will see you tomorrow, ja? And with *Gotte's* help, maybe we will finally have some answers."

Cheryl gulped. Of course her friend would understand what uncovering the truth meant. She was compassionate and supportive, but more than that, she truly cared for people. Cheryl returned her hug and then turned to Levi. Though he couldn't extend the same level of concern, the look in his eyes spoke volumes.

"I will see you tomorrow," he said, voice low.

"Okay," she said then immediately wished she'd been more articulate. She closed the door and slid the lock into place with a sigh. There was nothing for it…impressing him with her wit would have to wait until she wasn't so bogged down by worry and fatigue.

At her feet, Beau meowed, and Cheryl bent to gather him up.

"I know. I'm being silly, aren't I? My future with Levi has been decided, and I…well…I will just have to learn to live with it."

She scratched him under the chin and carried him with her to the bedroom. It had been a long day, but with thoughts of Levi running through her head, it threatened to be an even longer night. At least she would have Beau to keep her company.

She set him on the bed where he sat watching as she turned down the covers. Afterward, she slipped into the bathroom to wash and change and then padded to the bed to switch on the lamp.

"Okay, ready for bed?" she asked to no one in particular since the cat had disappeared.

"Beau?" She searched under the bed and around furniture. Catching movement from the corner of her eye, she turned toward the door just in time to see his tail swish from sight.

So much for having him for company, she thought, as she slid between the ice-cold sheets. Tonight the one thing she could count on was being alone.

CHAPTER TWELVE

Like most Amish families, the Bechnels kept a tidy farm with a well-tended yard and a large, two-story house painted crisp white. Shutters framed all of the lower windows, and a pea-gravel path wound up from the driveway toward a pretty gray porch. Cheryl climbed out of her car and waited until Levi and Naomi joined her before proceeding up the walk.

"So tell me again how Violet and Andrew wound up married?" she said under her breath. Naomi had shared a few details, but she wanted to make sure she had her facts straight before talking to Violet.

"Seth said he remembered Andrew resigning his position as police chief of Sugarcreek shortly after the Watters case concluded," Naomi said, her fingers reddened from clutching the edge of her cloak tightly under her chin. "There was even speculation for a while that Violet might leave the church in order to marry him, but Andrew would have none of it. He gave up his old life so the two of them could be together."

"He became Amish?"

Naomi's head bobbed. "They have been happily married ever since."

Their steps crunched almost in rhythm on the gravel drive. Cheryl slowed slightly and sensed when Levi did the same.

He bent his head toward her ear. "Are you all right?"

She huddled deeper into the warm folds of her coat and nodded. "Just worried, I guess. What if Violet tells us something about Uncle Ralph I don't want to hear?"

At the base of the steps, he pulled her to a halt and turned to face her. "Your onkel was an honorable man. If Violet knows something, it will only mean we will have to do a little more digging to figure out his motives."

There was no hesitation in his voice, no uncertainty in his steady blue gaze. The matter-of-fact words gave Cheryl the courage she needed to mount the steps and proceed to the door where Naomi waited.

"Ready?" she asked.

Cheryl nodded, and Naomi raised her hand to knock. It wasn't the Amish way—one simply entered a brethren's home, but she quickly realized it was a subtle warning to Violet that she and Levi were not alone. The door opened and Violet appeared, her eyes behind the thick glasses slightly troubled upon catching sight of them.

"Guder nammidaag, Naomi," she said, and then, "Hello, Cheryl. Levi. Please come in." She held the door wide and stepped back to allow them to enter. "I am surprised to see you this afternoon."

Oddly, though she spoke the words cheerfully, Cheryl didn't quite believe them. She met Violet's questioning stare steadily and was not surprised when she dropped her gaze.

Violet took their coats and then waved them farther into the wide, open room. A cheerful checkered sofa sat against one wall, and it was there that Violet led them. "Would you like to sit down?"

"Danki, Violet," Naomi said, her sensible shoes scuffing lightly across the carpeted floor.

She took a spot on the sofa. Cheryl sat next to her, and Levi claimed the opposite end. Across from them, Violet perched on the edge of a rust-colored wingback chair, her hands tightly clasped in her lap.

"What... um... what can I do for you?"

Cheryl sensed all eyes upon her, almost as if in deference to the fact that it was her family's reputation she had come to protect. Even Violet watched, her brown eyes round behind her glasses.

Cheryl cleared her throat, wishing she'd taken time to practice what she would say. Finally she decided the direct approach was best. "Violet, is it true that your last name used to be Watters?"

A blush colored Violet's cheeks, making them startlingly red against the white fabric of her kapp. "Who...?" She licked her lips and started again. "Who told you?" she whispered, her face pale.

"Was it a secret?" Cheryl countered.

Seconds ticked by, marked by a large wooden clock on the wall.

"I don't understand," Cheryl said, breaking the silence at last. "Why didn't you want anyone to know that you were Datschel and Trampas's sister?"

"I am not ashamed of Trampas," she corrected quickly, her bottom lip quivering.

Cheryl waited in stunned silence. Could it be possible that Violet believed Datschel guilty of murder?

She lifted her hand before anyone could speak. "Ne, it is not what you think."

"What do we think?" Naomi prompted quietly.

Violet's gaze shifted to her. "Before I tell you why I kept silent, it is important that you understand the suffering my family went through after Trampas drowned. It was more than just grief."

Tears filled Violet's eyes, and Cheryl felt empathy flicker to life inside her. "Tell us what happened, Violet," she said gently.

Next to her, she glimpsed Levi's head bow and sensed he was praying—not only for Violet, but her as well and everything she would learn about Uncle Ralph.

"My bruder, Trampas, he always had a restless way about him."

Violet's words came slow, like rusty wheels reluctant to turn, and then faster as she allowed them to break free.

"He was a good boy but so full of ambition." Her head dipped, and moisture glistened on her wrinkled cheek. "My daed had a different word for it. He called it pride, but no amount of chiding was enough to drive it from Trampas. He was like a dog with a bone when it came to his swimming. He just…refused to give it up no matter how much my father raged."

"Your father did not approve of him competing?" Cheryl asked. Though Jackson Mathers had already told her this, she wanted it confirmed by someone in the family.

Violet's head bobbed. "For Trampas, it was not enough just to swim. He had to win." Her hands fluttered up to her chin and balled into fists. "It was like he had a fire inside him, driving him to perform. My father did not understand it. And neither did I," she admitted sadly, "but I never viewed it the same way Daed did—as something to be reviled." Tears filled her eyes, and she sighed as she dropped her hands into her lap. "In a way, I think my father's disapproval only fueled Trampas's determination to compete. I think he believed if he did well enough, he might win more than a race. He would win our father's favor."

"And did he?" Levi asked.

Cheryl hadn't even realized he'd finished praying and was leaning forward to rest both elbows on his knees. Still, she wanted to know the answer, so she turned her attention back to Violet.

Her jawline hardened, and she shook her head. "My father died believing Trampas's death was a judgment from *Gott*," she said flatly. Her next words sounded choked from her. "He said his drowning was Gotte's way of showing that nothing should ever come before Him."

Cheryl stifled a gasp, but next to her, Naomi tsked softly.

"Surely he did not believe that Gott would act out of spite?"

"Not spite," Violet acknowledged quietly, turning her gaze to Naomi. "But a direct response to what he condemned as prideful behavior. My father believed that swimming had become an idol for Trampas, and that is why Gott took it away."

Her heavy sigh seemed drawn from the depths of her soul. She rose to pace, her hands wrinkling the fabric of her white cotton apron. "The Olympics…who would have thought such a thing could be possible for a young Amish boy? But then…a man came to Sugarcreek, someone who said he could find sponsors to help with Trampas's training."

She paused by a large picture window, the glow of which framed her shiver perfectly. "The argument that followed was so terrible. Trampas threatened to leave home, leave the church, an act which would have resulted in the ban. And Datschel...he was torn between him and my father."

She wiped tears from her eyes as she spoke and then pulled a handkerchief from a pocket of her apron to dry her nose.

"What about your mother?" Cheryl asked. "What did she have to say?"

"My mother died when we were young," Violet said. "Perhaps if she had been alive, playing the peacemaker would not have fallen to Datschel. As it was..."

She shrugged and wrapped her arms around her middle.

Levi cleared his throat. "So the day Trampas and your father fought...?"

She shuddered, as though the memory were too much for her to bear. "He drowned the same night." She pressed her hand to her chest and resumed pacing. "I think Datschel knew something bad was going to happen. He stormed from the house in search of Trampas even though Daed told him not to go." She ran knobby fingers over her face. "Later, when Datschel came home and told us what had happened..."

There was a long pause, during which she lifted her glasses with one hand and rubbed her eyes with the other. "I could hardly believe it—my bruder...dead. Even as the words came from Datschel's lips...I just...could not bring myself to believe they were true."

She looked at Cheryl, and her eyes filled with fresh tears. "Thank Gott your onkel was there to help us handle the media attention. All of a sudden there were reporters everywhere, in the yard and at the church. And the police. They even tried questioning my father." She trembled, remembering. "We never could have survived it had your onkel not stepped in."

Cheryl scooted to the edge of the sofa. "You said my uncle was there. Tell me about his involvement. The paper said he encouraged Datschel to keep silent until representation could arrive?"

"That is correct."

"Why?" she asked, a tad sharply. "Was it because he and your brother were friends, or was it something else?"

Cheryl forced herself to slow down and clutched her hands together tightly to lessen their shaking. At long last, she was talking to someone who remembered clearly what had happened all those years ago. But did she really want to hear what Violet had to say?

She licked her lips and tried again. "Your family must have known my uncle pretty well to have trusted him during such a difficult time."

"Of course. He had earned our trust."

"Do you mind telling me how?"

Violet resumed her seat in the chair, but her gaze was unfocused, as though she'd traveled far from this quaint farmhouse and was revisiting someplace from long ago. "It was during the later years of the war. There was so much trouble during that time. We were all affected by the number of people going off to fight. Friends and neighbors…"

She blinked and fastened her gaze on Cheryl. "A discussion arose about the Amish and our refusal to serve in the military. A handful—people who had lost loved ones overseas—questioned our right to abstain, but your onkel was one of the strongest voices of support. He was well respected in the community, so people listened to him, and the chatter soon died out. My father never forgot what he did—stepping forward in our defense."

Cheryl swallowed the thick knot that rose in her throat. Though she sensed Naomi's and Levi's support, this moment was only about Uncle Ralph and the great number of things she hadn't known about him. "So what happened?"

"He and my bruders became friends afterward," Violet said. "Daed too. They understood each other, I think. In some strange way, it was like a kinship of sorts existed between them. A couple of years later, I even heard Ralph trying to talk to my father about Trampas's swimming. It was the first and only time I ever heard them disagree."

Cheryl nodded sadly. "And your father? What happened to him?"

"He was different after Trampas died. Angry. Even bitter. He threatened to have him—his own son—buried outside the family cemetery as a way of showing others the consequences of his sin. He and Datschel argued terribly over it. Not long after, Datschel disappeared. I have not seen him since."

"And your father?" Cheryl asked quietly.

Now that the storm of emotion had passed, Violet seemed drained of strength. She sank into her chair, her shoulders stooped and her face lined with grief. "He died a few years later." Her head bowed, and she sniffled a moment before she was finally able to speak. "I think it was a combination of guilt and grief that took his life. He lost both of his sons the night Trampas drowned, even though it took longer for Datschel to slip away."

"*Es dutt mir leed*," Naomi whispered.

"I'm so sorry," Cheryl said in the same moment.

Violet nodded her thanks, but something in her demeanor was off. She turned her face away and refused to look at them. Her fingers clutched wrinkles into the fabric of her plain dress. And the line of her jaw was rigid, as though she fought to control the trembling of her lips.

Cheryl cast a glance at Levi. Perhaps Violet would be more inclined to talk without him present. He seemed to sense her unspoken request and rose to stand by the door.

"I will wait outside."

Thank you, Cheryl mouthed.

He nodded and slipped out the door.

Cheryl returned her attention to the sad woman hunched in the chair across from her. "Violet, why didn't you say something the day Naomi and I went to the library? Were you just reluctant to rehash everything that happened?"

Her head rose, and she peered steadily through her thick glasses. "Not reluctant. I was ashamed."

"Ashamed?" Naomi reached out to grasp her hand. "What do you have to be ashamed about? Every family has problems. Yours is no different."

She shook her head. "Ne, you do not understand. You see, I heard my father and Datschel arguing. I did not agree with Daed, but I did not speak up for fear that he would turn his anger toward me. Instead, I stood by while Datschel walked out the door, and I said nothing when my father yelled at him and told him never to return." Her chin quivered, but she pressed on. "He never did."

Tears rolled down her cheeks as she spoke. She took off her glasses and used the sleeve of her dress to wipe them away.

"His leaving was all my fault. Maybe if I had stood with him against my father...or at the very least told Datschel that I did not agree with his decision regarding Trampas..."

"Ne, Violet." Naomi lifted her chin adamantly, a move Cheryl recognized well. "He and your father fought, but leaving was Datschel's choice alone. As for why he stayed away..." Her shoulders drooped. "Only he can answer that question. Whatever the reason, I am confident it was not your fault."

Violet reached out and squeezed Naomi's hand in thanks and then extended her free hand to Cheryl. "I was wrong. I should have told you what I remembered about your onkel's involvement when I had the chance instead of letting you worry and wonder. I am sorry."

Cheryl took Violet's hand and gave it a squeeze back. "Actually, I sort of understand why you didn't speak up. I'm just...grateful that you spoke to us now."

Her cheeks reddened, and she dropped her gaze. "Danki."

"Can I ask you one more thing?"

Violet nodded.

"How did my uncle know that Trampas and your father fought? Uncle Ralph was at the river with Datschel when the police and media arrived, but how did he know where to go?"

Violet froze, and her features went blank. She lowered her gaze, and after a moment pulled her hand away and gave a slow shake of her head. "That is something... forgive me, Cheryl, but it is not my place to share."

"But..."

"Do not misunderstand," she urged quietly. "I do think you should know, but I am not the one to ask."

"Then who, Violet?" Naomi asked, her face looking as perplexed as Cheryl felt.

Violet's chin rose, and she fixed her eyes on Cheryl steadily. "You said your aunt Mitzi was going to be out of touch for a couple of weeks, ain't so?"

"Yes," Cheryl said hesitantly, confused by the sudden switch in topic. "But..."

"You should try to reach her, Cheryl," Violet said, her eyes shining and earnest. Her grasp on Cheryl's fingers tightened. "You should try to speak to her soon."

Chapter Thirteen

Naomi seemed to sense the weight pressing on Cheryl's spirit. She grasped her arm and gave it an encouraging squeeze when they arrived back in Sugarcreek.

"I am not sure you should be alone tonight," she said as they climbed from the car. "Maybe one of us should sit with you awhile."

"I couldn't ask..."

"I think that is a goot idea," Levi said, quelling the argument on Cheryl's tongue. "You have had a lot on your mind lately. I will take you for dinner and then see you home afterward."

Cheryl instantly felt a bit of the tension seep from her spine. She shot a grateful smile at Naomi and then slid her car keys into her pocket. "All right then. If you're sure?"

Levi swept his hand toward the street. "Where to?"

Naomi waved good-bye. Cheryl thought for a moment and, struck with an overwhelming craving for pepperoni, said hopefully, "Pizza?"

"Sounds goot."

"Are you sure? It's several blocks. We could drive."

He laughed and rubbed his hands together. "Walking is better. We will work off our pizza before we eat it."

He swung on to the sidewalk, his long strides shortened to match Cheryl's. "So what did you think of your visit with Violet?"

Cheryl puffed out a sigh. With temperatures starting to fall, she could see her breath lingering on the afternoon air. She shook her head. "It's a lot to take in. I guess the main thing will be to see about getting in touch with Aunt Mitzi. Maybe this evening. There's a large time difference between here and Papua New Guinea."

He blew on his fingers and then shoved his hands into his pockets.

Cheryl drew to a halt. "Listen, maybe this was a bad idea. It does feel like it's getting colder…"

Instead of stopping with her, Levi merely took her arm and pulled her along. After a couple of steps, he dropped his hand and grinned. "You need the distraction," he said. "So do I."

Cheryl wondered about that, but with her arm still warm where his hand had rested, she didn't argue. Though it was still early, dusk fell quickly in this part of the country in November. Cheryl snuggled deeper into the collar of her coat and enjoyed the brisk air, the cheery lights and sounds spilling from the storefronts and windows along Main Street, and the handsome man at her side. Too soon, the slanted roof of Park Street Pizza rolled into view.

"Here we are," Levi said, reaching to open the door for her and then allowing her to pass.

Inside, Cheryl was immediately greeted by the inviting scents of savory sauce and warm dough. She took a deep whiff and smiled as she reached for the buttons on her coat.

"This was a good choice," she said, fighting a small shiver of excitement when Levi's fingers brushed her shoulders as he helped her out of her coat.

"Levi! Cheryl! Over here."

Cheryl looked in the direction of the voice and smiled. "It's James and Grace." She waved at the couple from church and then turned to Levi. "Would you like to join them?"

He already wore a grin as he also waved. "Ja, that would be nice."

Park Street Pizza was not a large place, but it was popular, and people packed the tables. Cheryl wove her way toward the back of the restaurant and was greeted by a warm hug from Grace when she got there.

"This is a pleasant surprise. If we had known you two would be out, we'd have called and invited you."

Always bubbly, Grace didn't shy from wrapping Levi in an exuberant hug as well. Cheryl caught the slightly apologetic shrug James tossed at Levi before he motioned for them to sit.

"I'll fetch our waitress," James said, excusing himself.

Cheryl glanced at the plates already on the table. "Have you eaten?"

"Just an appetizer. We'll have plenty of pizza coming. Enough to share," Grace said, "assuming you like pepperoni?"

Both Cheryl and Levi nodded, and Grace propped her elbows on the table and rested her chin in her palms. "So what are you two up to? Not Christmas shopping already?" Her eyebrow quirked as she directed a pointed look at Cheryl.

"No, nothing like that," she replied hastily before Grace could run with the idea that she and Levi were doing something so personal as Christmas shopping together...or for each other. "We were actually working on a project for the Swiss Festival."

Grace's brow furrowed in confusion. "But we just finished with the festival last month. Do you mean next year?"

Cheryl nodded and quickly filled her in on the project the church was hoping to add to the festivities. By the time she finished, James had returned with their waitress and Levi ordered drinks for them both.

"Wow, that sounds really interesting," Grace said, picking at the top of her straw.

"It is," Cheryl said, "except that we've run across a few rabbit trails."

"What do you mean?"

She took a few more minutes to explain about the Watters case, during which time their food arrived. Unlike the Amish, Cheryl had learned the Mennonites at Friendship felt free to pray out loud publicly, and James led them in grace before they dug into their pies.

"So you really think your uncle played a part in everything that happened?" Grace said, wiping a bit of cheese off her chin.

Cheryl nodded. "I do. The problem is I'm not sure I'll be able to find out exactly what until I get ahold of Aunt Mitzi, which may not be for another week. They're out of cell phone range at the village where they're working."

"That's too bad," James said. "I mean about the cell phone range, not that they're working."

Grace covered his hand and shook her head at Cheryl. "Wait. Didn't you say you were using your uncle Ralph's old photos to help with the history project?"

She swallowed a bite of pizza. "Uh-huh."

Grace's gaze bounced from Cheryl to Levi. "Well?"

Confused, she glanced at Levi, who shrugged.

"Well what?"

"What if there's some clue to your uncle's connection to the Watters family in his stuff? I mean, he loved taking pictures, right? Some of those had to be of Datschel and Trampas."

Cheryl gaped. "The pictures…of course. Naomi suggested I dig through them, but I forgot all about it."

"Whoa." Levi laughed and held up his hand. "I know what you are thinking, Cheryl, but at least let me finish my pizza."

Cheryl joined in the laughter, although deep down, she really could not wait to get home to rummage through Uncle Ralph's things.

Grace's chatter increased as she caught a bit of Cheryl's excitement about searching for clues. "I'm certain you will find something in those old photos. Maybe we could stop by your house later and help you look?"

James quickly shook his head. "Don't forget we told your mother we would come by to help her dig a few of her Christmas decorations out of the attic."

"Oh, that's right," she said, her face falling glumly. "Mother always likes to get started early."

"I'll say." Cheryl laughed. "We haven't even had Thanksgiving."

Grace's lips turned in a wry grin. "Anyway, I'll be happy to stop by tomorrow if you want. That is, if you don't find anything tonight."

"Actually, that would be a huge help." Cheryl grimaced at the thought of the thousands of photos stuffed into the boxes she'd drug up from the basement. "Uncle Ralph had many hobbies, but photography was definitely his favorite."

"So tell me more about these Watters brothers." Grace stuffed another bite of pizza into her mouth then washed it down with a sip from her glass. "They were in their early twenties?"

"Around that," Cheryl said. "I don't know exactly how close in age they and Uncle Ralph were, but Trampas died over forty years ago, which would have made them at least twenty, if not older."

"Well, I guess there really isn't any way to check for sure since Amish people don't file birth records. But maybe James can find out something."

She turned to her husband and began drilling him with questions, but Cheryl's attention waned as she caught sight of a hunched figure in a familiar coat outside the Park Street Pizza window. She tapped Levi's arm and indicated the figure with a slight tip of her head.

"Is that Muddy?" she whispered.

He studied the man for a moment and then nodded. "It looks like him." He glanced at her, his eyebrows raised. "Is something wrong?"

His question arrested Grace's stream of chatter, and both she and James craned to see who they were discussing.

Grace pointed uncertainly. "Is that the homeless man everybody talks about around town?"

"I think so," James said. He turned to look at Cheryl. "Do you know him?"

"Not really," she admitted, and with a tinge of shame. She, like so many in Sugarcreek, only knew him as "that homeless man." Surely there was more to him than the title others had given him?

She pushed her chair back. "Will you all excuse me for a moment?"

"Cheryl, wait."

Levi made to rise, but she stopped him with a hand to his shoulder.

"It's all right. I just want to check on him...make sure he doesn't need anything. I'll be right back."

He still didn't look pleased, but finally, he nodded and motioned toward the window. "Stay where we can see you, ja?"

His protectiveness made her insides melt. She nodded in mute agreement then grabbed her coat and wound toward the exit. Before stepping outside, she tossed one last glance toward the table. Three pairs of eyes watched her curiously, but only one also shone with something deeper than concern.

Gulping a breath of brisk air, she slid her arms into her coat and then ducked through the door. By this time, Muddy had shuffled a ways up the street, but she quickly caught up to him.

"Muddy?"

He kept moving, so Cheryl called again.

"Muddy, is that you?"

This time he paused. After a bit, his shoulder turned, and Cheryl caught a glimpse of his face from the glow of the street lamps.

"Evening, Miss Cooper."

"I thought that was you." Cold air seeped past Cheryl's collar. She shivered and hugged herself tight. "What are you doing out so late?"

He held up a bag stamped with the Park Street Pizza logo. "I come by from time to time. The owners save pizza for me when they can."

Cheryl nodded and tossed a glance up toward the sky. "It's a clear night out. Feels a little chilly. Will you be all right tonight?"

He offered a crooked grin and ran his hand down the length of his coat. "I will now, thanks to you."

"What about...?" Her face warmed with embarrassment. Unable to think of a subtle way of asking her question, she opted for the direct approach. "Muddy, where will you sleep? Do you have someplace to go, or...do you need a place?"

For a moment he looked confused, but then this brow cleared and he hitched his thumb over his shoulder. "I'll catch a ride to one of the homeless shelters nearby. They fill up fast though. I should probably go. You take care, Miss Cooper."

"You too, Muddy."

Concern pressed on her heart. He had food and a place to sleep. Thanks to her church's clothing closet, he also had a coat. But what about tomorrow or the day after that? What would he do for the long number of days stretching between now and warmer spring temperatures?

Behind her, the door to Park Street Pizza creaked open and noise and laughter spilled out from inside, but she didn't turn. She knew instinctively it was Levi and that he stood watching her with the same look of intense concern she'd witnessed on his face earlier. She felt his urging her to return, sensed his hesitance and unspoken questions.

Despite the love and concern she felt emanating from Levi, Cheryl didn't turn. Instead, she watched as a thin figure draped in a coat that was slightly too large disappeared from view.

CHAPTER FOURTEEN

Cheryl grabbed another box of photos off of the stack she'd dragged up from the basement and gave a sigh of frustration that riffled the spiky tips of her bright red hair.

Nothing.

She'd searched through hundreds of photos into the wee hours last night and had resumed looking the moment she got home after the Swiss Miss closed today. Her eyes felt like sandpaper, her fingers bore too many paper cuts to count, and she was fighting the beginnings of a headache, and what did she have to show for it?

Nothing.

At least... nothing that matched her photo of Datschel. She *had* learned her uncle had a knack for capturing tender moments during weddings. And she knew he had a thing for photographing horses and buggies, as they appeared in image after countless image. But Datschel and Trampas Watters?

She sighed again and was more than just slightly relieved when a knock sounded on her door a split second before she broke open another box.

"Coming!"

She straightened and took a moment to rub the tightness from her back and shoulders before picking her way through the maze of boxes spread out on the floor. Grace had mentioned stopping by, so she was a little surprised when she opened the door and found Naomi waiting on her front step. A dusting of powdery snow covered her bonnet and cloak, and her breath spiraled in feathery wisps above her head.

"Cheryl, goot. I am glad you are home." She stomped her feet, a move that likely did little to ward off the frigid fingers ruffling her hem.

"Naomi…my goodness. Come in, come in." Cheryl stepped back to let her pass then quickly closed the door on an icy blast pressing to get in. "It certainly has gotten colder this evening."

"Ja. The men are all saying we will see heavy snow by late tonight or early tomorrow. I am glad we finished closing up the corn maze and petting zoo last week."

She shrugged out of her coat and placed it in Cheryl's waiting hands.

"Danki."

"Come into the kitchen," Cheryl said. "I'll get you something warm to drink."

Riding in an Amish buggy in the winter was certainly different than riding in the summer, she thought as she hung Naomi's cloak and then led the way to the kitchen. The buggy robes the family used to cover their legs in winter were beautiful and warm, but they did not compare to a car heater on full blast.

She reached for her coffee tin and set about starting a pot to brew. "What are you doing out on such a chilly evening? If the men are talking snow, surely Seth will be concerned?"

"Seth had to make a trip into town. I came with him because I wanted to see you," Naomi explained, blowing on her reddened fingers. "What did you find out?"

"About Uncle Ralph?" She grimaced. "So far, not much, other than a few tidbits regarding his favorite hobby."

She measured another scoop of coffee grounds into a filter then grabbed the carafe and filled it with water. "Did Levi tell you we ran into James and Grace last night?"

She nodded. "Ja. He said Grace also suggested looking for a clue in Ralph's old boxes."

"She did, and I'm glad because I forgot all about it. So far, that has pretty much been a dead end." Cheryl poured the water into the coffeemaker's tank then mashed the Brew button. "Looking through those old pictures is actually much harder than I thought. A lot of them are taken from behind, so all I really see is the person's back and the scenery beyond. Others are too far away for me to make anyone out clearly. Looks like I will have to wait on Aunt Mitzi after all."

"I am sorry, Cheryl. I know you were hoping to learn something sooner." Naomi gestured toward the living room. "Can I help you look?"

"I wouldn't mind the help," Cheryl said hesitantly, "but are you sure you have time?"

She gave a quick nod. "Seth has several errands to run so I know he will be at least an hour, probably two. Anyway, I told him to meet me here when he is finished, so it is no problem."

Cheryl immediately felt her mood brighten. "Great. Thank you, Naomi. I really appreciate the offer."

The aroma of fresh coffee quickly filled the kitchen. Cheryl waited for the pot to finish dripping before pouring herself and Naomi a cup. They carried them to the living room, and Cheryl explained which boxes she had searched and which ones she had yet to look through.

"Well, it appears you have a good start. You are almost halfway through the boxes."

Cheryl set her cup down with a groan. "I wish. There are more boxes downstairs. I just figured I'd get through these first before going back for more."

"Oh my." Naomi tapped her finger on her chin. "Then I suppose we should get started."

She set her cup next to Cheryl's then bent to pull the nearest box closer. Cheryl too grabbed a box but was stopped from digging into it by the ringing of her cell phone.

"I'll be right back," she said, jumping up to answer it.

It took her several seconds to find her phone, but when she did, the display showed Grace's name and number. Cheryl snatched it up off the kitchen counter and said hello.

"Cheryl? It's me, Grace."

"Hi, Grace."

"Have you found anything?" she said, cutting straight to the purpose of her call.

"Not yet," Cheryl said. Sensing the disappointment that emanated from her phone, she added, "Naomi and I were just about to look through another stack of boxes. Are you coming by?"

"I can't," Grace said, a pout in her voice that made Cheryl smile. "That's why I'm calling. Well, that and to see if you'd found anything juicy."

They laughed, and then Grace went on.

"I really did intend to stop by earlier, but James's sister called and needed me to babysit. She and her husband do so much for us, I couldn't tell her no. I'm so sorry."

"Don't even worry about it," Cheryl assured her quickly. "I hope everything is okay?"

"Oh yes, everything is fine. Listen, I could come over tomorrow, if you think you'll still need a hand, that is."

Cheryl thought for a moment and then shook her head. "Tell you what, if we come up empty tonight, I'll give you a call."

"That will work."

"Great. Thanks for calling, Grace."

"You bet. And Cheryl? I really do hope you figure out what happened with your uncle."

Cheryl thanked her, they chatted a bit more before saying good-bye, and then she returned to the living room to sit alongside Naomi.

For nearly half an hour, both she and Cheryl worked in silence, sorting through old photos and exclaiming over things they remembered or things they didn't. Finally, her coffee cup drained, Cheryl rose.

"I'm going to refill my cup. Would you like some more?"

She smiled at Naomi's absentminded agreement. Apparently, though many Amish people were not comfortable having their picture taken, they had no objection to looking at them once they were finished. Suddenly, Cheryl realized what that meant.

She looked around the cottage. On one wall, photos of her father and mother hung alongside family photos with her and her brother Matt as children. On the fireplace mantel, a beautifully framed wedding photo of Aunt Mitzi and Uncle Ralph sat alongside individual pictures of the two of them as young adults.

And in her parents' home back in Seattle, she couldn't think of a single room that wasn't dominated by pictures of her and Matt in various stages of age and growth—from baby pictures to graduation.

Naomi had none of these.

Cheryl set the empty cups down and resumed her seat next to Naomi. Their task momentarily forgotten, she bent to see what her friend was studying so intently. They were photos of Amish children, taken mostly from the back or in profile.

"Are you looking for something?" she asked gently.

Naomi startled and then set the photos aside almost contritely. "Ach, I am sorry, Cheryl. I am afraid I allowed myself to get distracted."

Cheryl picked up the pictures she'd discarded. She slid one out from the stack and held it up for a closer study. "This one almost looks like Esther," she said, handing it back to Naomi.

Naomi took the photo and held it gently between her fingers. "Ja, I thought so too."

"Are you sad that you don't have any pictures of the children when they were younger?"

She ducked her head, effectively hiding her eyes but unable to do anything about the trembling of her chin. Cheryl covered her hand with her own and gave a squeeze.

Naomi squeezed back. Finally, her head lifted. Though her eyes looked red, she offered a small smile. "It is silly really. It is just that, as I have gotten older, I have realized how fleeting the years have grown. And how quickly my *kinder* are becoming adults. Soon they will all be married and have families of their own."

She sighed and handed the photo back to Cheryl.

"It is not that I do not wish for my children to be happy," she continued. "It is just that sometimes I think on the days when Esther and the others were *bopplis* and wish for that time back, but it cannot be. No photos will ever regain the years that have passed. But it would be nice to be able to revisit them again...every once in a while," she added.

Her wry smile faded, replaced by something closer to remorse. She laid her hands in her lap, her fingers clasped so tightly she turned the skin over her knuckles white. "And I cannot help but think of Levi, Caleb, and Sarah. Though it has been many years since they said so, I know they still miss their maam. I wonder sometimes if they do not wish they had a photo of her, of Ruth, to remember her by."

What could she say to that? Cheryl bit her lip and remained silent.

Finally, Naomi clapped her hands to her knees and blew out another sigh. "Enough reminiscing, ja? Time to get back to work."

Without waiting for an answer, she reached for the box, signaling that she'd said all she wanted to about old photos.

Cheryl rose and made for the kitchen. Here again was another difference between her life and Levi's. Was this God's way of showing her that they were not meant to be together? After all, if they could not reconcile something so insignificant as family photos, how would they broach the differences in their faith?

She took her time refreshing their cups, and by the time she went back to the living room, Naomi had moved on to another box and was shoving it against the wall with the ones already finished.

"This one does not have photos," she explained. "Only books."

"Oh? What kind of books?"

"Picture books but not the kind your uncle would have taken." She lifted the flap on the box so Cheryl could look inside.

"Those are yearbooks," she exclaimed and lifted one out. "These are pretty old. This one goes back to 1961."

Naomi gently ran her finger over the spine of the next book in the box. "What is a yearbook?"

"Ah, right. You don't have these." Cheryl flipped open the cover. "Yearbooks are a sort of picture history book of the school where they were made. See this here?" She pointed to the name and address printed on the first page. "This is the high school Uncle Ralph attended."

Her eyes flashed with interest. "So is your uncle Ralph in this yearbook?"

"Actually..." Cheryl fanned through the pages of the yearbook. "I'm not sure. I don't know the exact year that he graduated." She did a quick mental calculation and nodded. "Yeah, I think this would be about the right time. Uncle Ralph was in his late sixties when he passed away, which means he would have been in his teens in 1961. Let's look."

Surprisingly, there were many names in the yearbook that Cheryl recognized. She and Naomi laughed and exclaimed over many of the photos, none of which contained Uncle Ralph.

At the last page, Naomi folded the book closed and laid it aside. "Ach, well, that was all very entertaining but...are there any later books in the box? Perhaps if we tried another year?"

"I'll check," Cheryl said, digging through almost half of the box before she found one from 1964. She held it aloft. "Here's one. This one definitely has to have pictures of Uncle Ralph."

Indeed, there were many photos of him—on the basketball team, holding a football, there was even one of him in a theater production, which was entirely surprising since Cheryl had always known her uncle to be rather shy.

"He was a very handsome young man," Naomi said, her eyes twinkling. "I can see what your aunt Mitzi found so appealing."

Cheryl couldn't help but laugh. "I agree, he was quite a looker, but it sure sounds weird thinking of my aunt and uncle being young and in love."

She flipped the page to a collage of photos, many of which featured her uncle with an attractive brunette on his arm.

Naomi bent close to examine one of them. "Your aunt Mitzi was a very beautiful woman. I do not mean she is not beautiful now. It is just...I hardly recognize her here." She tapped the page with her finger and turned the book for Cheryl to see.

Cheryl squinted, trying to make out the face in the photo. "No, that can't be. I mean, I do remember Aunt Mitzi being quite pretty in her younger days, but..."

She squinted harder. "This is really odd."

She flipped several more pages. Time and again, where there were group photos that included Uncle Ralph, a pretty brunette stood close by his side.

"Cheryl, are you looking for something?" Naomi asked, watching with a perplexed frown as she began turning the pages faster.

"No...well...it's just..."

She stopped and laid the book open for Naomi to see. "Aunt Mitzi was pretty, Naomi. The problem is"—she jabbed her finger at one of the photos of Uncle Ralph with the pretty brunette on his arm—"this isn't her."

Chapter Fifteen

"Well, these photos *were* taken many years ago," Naomi began, but Cheryl cut her off with an adamant shake of her head.

"No. Absolutely not. Aunt Mitzi moved to Sugarcreek after she and Uncle Ralph married, so this *can't* be her in the yearbook photos. The problem is I very clearly remember Aunt Mitzi telling me that Uncle Ralph never really dated in high school. He was sort of shy, I guess, and didn't feel comfortable with girls his own age, which is why he never saw anyone seriously until he met Aunt Mitzi."

Naomi spun the yearbook around and stared at the faces of the young couple printed on the page. "So then if Ralph did not date, who is this woman?"

"There's one way to find out," Cheryl said.

Backing up to the beginning of the book, she began scanning through all of the class photos until she found one that matched.

"That's her!" she said excitedly.

She ran her finger across the page to the names printed neatly in a column. "Darren Boggs, Pam Perry, Alexander Price, Mazee…"

She broke off, stunned.

"Who is it?" Naomi said. She grabbed the book and ran her finger the same way across the page. "Mazee Vander Huis." She looked up at Cheryl. "You know this woman?"

"Not as Vander Huis," Cheryl whispered. "I thought the woman's face looked familiar. Now I know why. The woman in the photos with Uncle Ralph is Mazee Stillwell."

Naomi's mouth formed a round O. "Stillwell—the woman from your church? The one who is supposed to help you with the history project?"

Cheryl nodded. "That's her."

Her eyes rounded as she took another glimpse of the photo in the yearbook. "I did not realize she and your uncle were so close."

"Neither did I, and neither did Aunt Mitzi, apparently." Cheryl swallowed a large knot in her throat.

Seeing her discomfort, Naomi reached out and patted her hand. "I am sure there is a simple explanation. Either Mitzi just forgot to tell you about Mazee, or she and Ralph were not dating as it appears and were just very goot friends."

Instant relief washed over Cheryl. She straightened and blew out a nervous sigh. "Of course. Either one of those are possible. I guess it just took me by surprise, seeing pictures of Uncle Ralph with someone else." She gave an embarrassed chuckle. "Sorry. I shouldn't have made such a big deal out of it."

"Do not worry. It was an easy mistake to make." Naomi closed the yearbook firmly and handed it back to Cheryl. "But jumping to conclusions is not nearly as good an exercise as digging for facts. Perhaps we should keep looking."

"Agreed." Cheryl set the yearbook aside, yet her eyes returned to it again and again until finally she picked it up and carried it back to the box she'd pulled it from. "Think I'll just take a couple of these downstairs so we don't get them confused with the ones we still have to look through."

She didn't wait for Naomi's reply, but bent to pick up the box and was surprised when she felt the bottom flap giving way.

"Oh...oh no!"

She did a crazy sort of juggling act, but it was too late and the books were too heavy. The bottom ripped loose and the yearbooks tumbled out, most of which whacked Cheryl's foot before thumping on the floor. She gave a sharp cry of pain and began hopping wildly on one foot.

"Cheryl, are you all right?" Naomi leaped to her feet and scrambled to grasp her elbow to keep her from falling over.

"Ow...oh, my toe," Cheryl cried, real tears pooling in her eyes.

"Maybe you should sit down," Naomi instructed. She led Cheryl to a chair and then hurried off toward the kitchen. "Stay there. I will fetch some ice."

By the time she returned, the throbbing in Cheryl's foot had lessened to something a smidge below piercing, but she applied the ice pack thankfully and accepted the tissue that Naomi pressed into her hand.

"How is it?" Naomi bent to touch her foot gingerly. "Does it feel broken?"

"I don't think so." Cheryl straightened her leg and cautiously wiggled her toes. "But I'm pretty sure my foot will be black and blue tomorrow. Who would have thought those books could be so heavy...or dangerous?"

She grimaced and replaced the ice pack.

"I am just glad it happened before you started down the stairs." A shudder shook Naomi's shoulders. "You could have been seriously hurt."

"That's true. Those stairs are pretty steep. I guess I should be glad it's just a bruise." Cheryl sniffed and wiped the tears from her eyes while Naomi set about gathering up the yearbooks.

"It must be the dampness in the basement that caused the cardboard to weaken," she said, stacking the books one atop the other. "You had better be careful before bringing up any more boxes."

Cheryl shrugged. "It'll probably be okay. I'm sure it's just because that one was so heavy."

Now that the ice had numbed some of the pain, she no longer felt quite so helpless. She reached out to push a couple of the scattered yearbooks toward Naomi but stopped when a note scribbled inside the cover of one of them caught her eye.

"'To Ralph,'" she read out loud.

Naomi's head lifted as she listened.

Scooting to the edge of her chair, she craned her neck to see. "'You are the only person who could truly make me smile. All my love, Mazee.'" Cheryl met Naomi's gaze over the edge of the yearbook. "That's pretty strong language for two people who were just friends."

"Now, Cheryl…"

Naomi raised a finger in warning, but Cheryl didn't listen. She grabbed an older book and began flipping through the pages. This one bore a similar message:

To Ralph, You're a very special person. I will always
treasure our time together.

With all my love, Mazee

But it was the last book Cheryl looked through, the one
containing Mazee's and Ralph's senior pictures, which troubled her
the most. Inside was a message that made her face warm:

To Ralph, with my undying gratitude and devotion. I
will always love you. I hope you can forgive me.

Mazee

Her fingers shook as she closed the book. "They were more
than just friends, Naomi."

Naomi's face grew solemn. "Perhaps we should wait and ask
your aunt Mitzi before we presume to know how close Mazee and
Ralph were."

"What if she didn't know? What if she never realized Uncle
Ralph cared for anyone else?"

Naomi frowned uncertainly. "I do not...what are you
suggesting, Cheryl? You think your uncle Ralph purposely did not
tell your aunt about Mazee? Why would he do that?"

Maybe because he still had feelings for Mazee? Cheryl frowned,
thinking. "There is one person who could tell me what happened
between them, and it might explain why she was unwilling to talk
about Datschel and Trampas Watters."

"Mazee Stillwell?"

Cheryl nodded. "What are the chances that the two things are connected?"

Neither of them spoke or blinked. Finally, Cheryl broke the standoff. "Okay, so I think I need to pay another visit to Mazee."

"You will not go tonight?"

Naomi cast a worried glance toward the window. Fat snowflakes had begun collecting on the sill, and a breeze had kicked up and stirred the branches visible in the glow from the lamp. Cheryl sighed and hugged the yearbook to her chest. Naomi was right, conditions were worsening outside. And that meant any questions she had for Mazee would have to wait until morning.

The first snowfall of the season turned out to be more bluff than bluster. It snowed just enough to coat the ground in white, a blanket that quickly melted away with the rising of the sun. Cheryl counted the hours until lunch, when Esther took over and she and Naomi were able to scoot out the door and head for Mazee's house.

"I'm glad you agreed to come with me, Naomi." Cheryl loosened her grip on the steering wheel and glanced sidelong at her friend. "The more I thought about talking to Mazee about Uncle Ralph, the more anxious I got."

"It is no trouble. I am glad to help if I can," she assured. Her smile slowly drooped into a frown. "Cheryl, do you think maybe we should go by your house and pick up the newspaper articles you found on Datschel and Trampas?"

She removed her foot from the gas. "I hadn't thought about it. Why?"

"Well, Mazee may have been reluctant to talk about it too much before, but if she knows that you are aware of her relationship with Ralph, perhaps she might be a little more forthcoming."

Cheryl thought for a second and then hit her blinker and prepared to turn. "*Hmm*...you're right. We probably should be prepared, just in case. But I can't go by the house. I took the photos Mazee gave me to the church so I could get copies made. The articles and other things from the library are in the same bag with Mazee's envelope. I need to return her things anyway, so it's probably a good idea to stop and pick them up. We'll swing by there on our way to Mazee's."

Naomi agreed, and a few minutes later, they pulled into the parking lot.

"I'll run in real quick and check the office," Cheryl said, taking off her seat belt. "Kelly, our church secretary, said she would leave a packet for me by the door."

But a quick check of the office didn't reveal the expected packet. Cheryl frowned as she peered through the office window. Apparently, the office staff were on their lunch break. If they'd left at the same time as she and Naomi, they probably wouldn't be back for almost an hour.

"Great," Cheryl mumbled. "I knew I should have called first."

Almost out of habit, her hand fell to the doorknob, and she was both surprised and hopeful when it turned. Maybe she wasn't out of luck after all. Maybe Kelly had meant she would leave the packet inside the door instead of next to it.

She pushed open the door and stuck her head into the office. "Hello?"

Not receiving an answer, she moved farther in and took a quick glance around. There was no envelope on the desk, and no Kelly. On the slim chance the packet had been left next to the copier, Cheryl wound through the church office toward the copy room, located near the back and in a smaller room off the hall. The lights had been turned off, but enough sunlight trickled through the window blinds for Cheryl to spy a strange curl of something that looked like smoke coming from under the door.

She quickened her steps, certain as she drew closer that what she saw...and smelled...was smoke.

Heart pounding, she yelled for Naomi and then frowned. There was no way she was going to hear her calling outside the building and in her car. She ran back the few steps to the entrance and waved frantically until she got her attention.

Naomi stepped hesitantly out of the car. "Cheryl?"

"Come quick. I think something's burning!"

Shock registered on Naomi's face, and then she ran to meet Cheryl at the door. "You saw a fire? Should we call the fire department?"

"Not a fire. Smoke."

"Where?"

"Back here, by the copy room."

She raced back the way she'd come but was shocked when they got there to see the door standing open and a wall of smoke billowing out. Her first thought was of the church secretary.

"Kelly?"

Clunking ensued, followed by stomping that seemed much too loud and heavy to be caused by their petite church secretary. Cheryl took a hesitant step forward and was almost bowled over when a large figure holding a smoking trash can emerged from the copy room.

"Muddy?"

"Step aside, Miss Cooper!"

Muddy held the trash can aloft, arms extended to keep the worst of the smoke from wafting into his face. A second later, the smoke detector went off, adding its frantic chirping to the chaos.

"Take it outside!" Naomi hurried back to the door and held it open for him then waved him through. Coughing and sputtering, Muddy deposited the trash can on the sidewalk.

Cheryl rushed to his side and began patting his back helplessly. "Are you all right? What happened in there?"

Muddy doubled over to rest his hands on his knees. His eyes were watering, and his face looked warm . . . too warm.

"Stay right here. I'm going to find you some water." Cheryl ran back inside to the office, where a heavy cloud of smoke still lingered. She opened a couple of windows, and then, spying a water cooler, she poured a glass and rushed back outside where Naomi and Muddy waited.

He no longer gagged, but Muddy still struggled to catch his breath. He took a long drink from the glass then swiped his sleeve across his eyes. "Thank you."

Next to him, the trash can was still smoldering, but there were no flames, so whatever had caught fire had apparently burned itself out.

"What happened?" Cheryl asked again, her voice a trifle shaky. Her gaze dropped to Muddy's hands. "You didn't burn yourself, did you?"

He straightened, still coughing a bit, but definitely looking better. "No, ma'am. I'm fine."

"What happened?" This time it was Naomi who asked.

Muddy shook his head. "No idea. I heard Miss Cooper calling, and then I saw smoke coming from under the door." He jabbed his thumb toward the church. "I just happened to come by because...well...sometimes there's an envelope for me in the office."

"An envelope?" Cheryl asked.

His large feet began to shuffle, and he dropped his gaze. "Yeah...uh...with money."

"Oh." Cheryl felt bad for having embarrassed him and decided to shift the topic back to the fire. "I'm really glad you were here, Muddy, but how did you get into the church? Naomi and I didn't see you come in the front door."

He shook his head. "No, ma'am. I came through the gym doors, around the back."

"They were unlocked?"

His face flushed an even deeper red. "Miss Kelly usually leaves them open for me during the day so I can clean up, use the showers, and whatnot."

Cheryl glanced at Naomi. There *were* showers in the gym, but she had no idea that the church allowed people to come in to use them at will, especially when no one was in the office. She'd have to make a point of asking Kelly about it.

Cheryl gestured to the trash can, which no longer smoldered, but which now had permanently blackened sides. "So you didn't see what started this?"

Muddy shook his head. "'Fraid not. Like I said, I heard you yelling and come runnin'."

She glanced at the charred remains lying in the bottom of the trash can. "Wait. Is that…?" Dismayed, she bent and tugged at a corner of something poking up through the ashes. "This is the envelope I got from Mazee."

"What?" Naomi drew near to examine the bit of paper. "Cheryl, are you sure?"

"Positive." Her stomach sank as she peered into the trash can. "There's nothing left. My folder, the pictures, it's all gone."

Naomi nudged the trash can with her toe. "I do not understand. Why would anyone want to burn your things?"

Cheryl glanced at the doors to the church. "And how did they know to come now, when everyone was gone?" She stared first at Naomi and then at Muddy, who seemed to have grown as confused as she felt… and twice as uncomfortable. He tugged at the edge of his coat and looked at the trash can, the church, everywhere but at her.

Suspicion rooted in Cheryl's head. She narrowed her eyes and crossed both arms over her chest. "Muddy, are you sure you didn't see anything?"

His gaze swung to her, but this time there was a sadness lurking there that made her squirm.

"I am sure, Miss Cooper, but I understand if you don't believe me."

By now Cheryl had practically tuned out the screeching of the smoke alarm, but the blare of the fire truck as it rumbled into the parking lot off of the street definitely caught her attention.

She looked at Naomi. "Did you call 911?"

She shook her head. "Ne. The fire alarm must have triggered a call."

Muddy suddenly looked uncomfortable. He rolled one shoulder and took a step toward the sidewalk. "Well, if you don't need me anymore, I suppose I'd best be going. I'm real sorry about your stuff."

Cheryl blinked, awash with guilt for having implied that he might be lying when he'd given her no cause to think so. "Muddy, wait."

But it was too late. His long gait had already carried him to the end of the sidewalk. Before she could call him back, he rounded the corner and disappeared.

Chapter Sixteen

Though she wanted to go after Muddy, Cheryl knew she needed to speak to the firefighters climbing down from the fire truck.

"Hey there, is everything all right?" one of them called.

Cheryl and Naomi crossed to them, quickly explained what had happened, and then waited while they went inside the church to make sure nothing else had been affected by the blaze.

While they checked, Cheryl called Kelly. A short while later, she and Pastor Lory arrived. Both looked as perplexed as Cheryl felt as to what could have caused the fire. All four waited huddled on the sidewalk until the firefighters returned and gave them the all clear.

"Looks like whatever caused the fire was contained to the trash can," another of the firefighters said. "Was anyone using matches, by chance?"

"I don't think...," Pastor Lory began.

"Actually, yes," Kelly interrupted him. Embarrassment reddened her cheeks. "I lit a candle earlier today, but it never occurred to me that throwing the match in the trash could start a fire. I'm so sorry."

So that explained the fire, but what about her pictures? Cheryl waited until the fire trucks had gone and Pastor Lory ducked inside the church before approaching Kelly.

"I'm so ashamed," Kelly said, lowering her voice. "How could I have done something so irresponsible?"

Cheryl patted her arm compassionately. "Don't be too hard on yourself, Kelly."

"Ja. It was an accident, pure and simple," Naomi added.

Kelly didn't seem convinced. She blinked, struggling against tears. "Well, anyway, I'm glad you both stopped by before the fire got any worse."

"Me too," Cheryl said. She cleared her throat uncomfortably. "Say, Kelly, would you mind telling me how my pictures ended up in the trash can?"

"What?" Kelly stared at her, clearly puzzled. "I didn't put your pictures in the trash. I knew you were coming, so I left them by the door, just like I said."

Cheryl and Naomi shared a glance.

"You mean they aren't there?" She moved as if to check, a frown on her lips.

Cheryl stopped her before she could go inside. "I'm sure they're gone, Kelly. We found pieces of them among the ashes."

"But that can't be." Her voice rose a notch, and she hurried over to the trash can to look inside. "I know I put those pictures by the door for you. I even checked before I left for lunch. How did they end up in here?"

How indeed? Cheryl spent several minutes assuring Kelly that she wasn't angry, nor did she blame her for what had happened. Though they did not have an answer for what had occurred, she was at least certain that the poor church secretary didn't hold herself responsible when they left.

"Well, we have completely managed to waste an afternoon," Cheryl grumbled as she and Naomi returned to the parking lot. She stomped her foot against the cold pavement then immediately regretted the action when pain shot from her toe up to her ankle. "Ouch! Sugar and grits, that hurt."

Naomi hastened toward her. "Are you all right?"

Cheryl groaned and bent to rub her throbbing foot. "I'm all right. I just forgot about dropping those books on my toe."

She sighed and glared at the trash can still sitting blackened and forlorn on the sidewalk.

"Well, I suppose I might as well head back to the store and drop you off, Naomi. I'll have to tell Mazee about her pictures, but you don't need to be with me for that."

Naomi frowned. "Aren't you going to ask her about Datschel and Trampas?"

"Why would I? All of the articles are gone. I'd have to go by the library to reprint everything."

Naomi gave a stubborn shake of her head. "Ne. I do not think you should let this stop you." She waved at the trash can. "If anything, this proves that somebody does not want you digging into the past."

Cheryl straightened and eyed the trash can skeptically. "You think so?"

"Why else would they go to the trouble to burn the evidence?"

She let that thought sink in for a minute then brightened and gave a determined nod. "You're right, Naomi. I say we go ahead and pay a visit to Mazee Stillwell, if you're still up to it."

"I am up to it." Her chin rose, and her eyes shone bright. "Let us go see what she has to say."

Cheryl agreed, and before long they were on the road heading toward Mazee's. Despite having told Naomi she didn't have to come, Cheryl was glad to have her along when they pulled up to the Stillwell Mansion. Mazee's gray SUV sat in the driveway, and this time it was Mazee herself who answered the door. As always, she looked sleek in a pair of black slacks and matching sweater, but something in her manner made Cheryl think they'd caught her just as she'd been about to leave.

Cheryl pasted a bright smile to her lips and extended her hand. "Good afternoon, Mazee."

"Cheryl!"

"I hope you don't mind our stopping by. Did we catch you at a bad time?"

Mazee looked a little flustered as she took Cheryl's hand and returned the greeting. "No, of course not." She gave a breathless chuckle. "I just wasn't expecting you. Actually, I was coming to see if any packages had been left on the step. I'm expecting an order today. Imagine my surprise when I opened the door and found you standing there." She pressed her hand to her heart. "Give an old lady a heart attack."

Cheryl smiled in apology. "I'm so sorry. I probably should have called first."

She seemed to collect herself with effort. Her smile returned, and she gave a gracious shake of her head. "Not at all, dear. I'm glad to see you." Her gaze drifted past Cheryl. "And who is your friend?"

"This is Naomi Miller. Naomi, meet Mazee Stillwell."

Instead of extending her hand, Mazee slid them behind her back. She dipped her head in an old-fashioned kind of way that reminded Cheryl of the ladies of Barton Cottage, only with none of the romantic sensibility. "It's a pleasure to meet you, Mrs. Miller."

"You as well. And please call me Naomi."

"Of course. And call me Mazee." She invited them inside and then led them to the same drawing room where she and Cheryl first spoke. Once they were all seated, she turned to Cheryl and offered a bright smile.

"So? How is the history project coming? Were you able to use some of the photos I gave you?"

Cheryl squirmed uncomfortably in her chair. "Actually, that's why we're here. I'm afraid I have some bad news."

Her eyebrows rose. "Oh?"

"Yes. I had planned on using some of the pictures you gave me, quite a few of them, in fact. But I'm afraid that won't be possible now."

Her lips puckered into a frown. "Why is that?"

Though the fire was in no way her fault, Cheryl felt awash with a sudden wave of embarrassment. "I'm afraid someone burned them."

"What?" Mazee exclaimed. "Why would anyone do that?"

Feeling prompted to explain, Cheryl leaned forward and sucked in a breath. "I'm so sorry, Mazee. I dropped them off at the church office for copies, but when Naomi and I went by earlier today to pick them up, we discovered someone had gotten there before us."

Mazee's mouth opened and shut, and she plucked at the sleeve of her plain black sweater. "But...that is just so..."

"Strange? Suspicious? Alarming? Yes, it is," Cheryl said. She spread her hands wide. "Again, I am so sorry. Those pictures have to be irreplaceable. I don't know how I'll ever make it up to you."

"No, no." Mazee gave an adamant shake of her head. "Please don't worry about that. I'm just so glad that you are okay." She turned to look at Naomi. "Were you there as well?"

"I was," Naomi said, "but it was Cheryl who found the fire, and Muddy who put it out."

"The homeless man?" Mazee said carefully. "What on earth was he doing there?"

Cheryl felt uncomfortable sharing his reasons, so she praised him instead. "Well, we're just grateful he happened by. He heard me call out and stepped in very quickly to help."

Mazee seemed to accept this. She blew out a relieved sigh. "Well, I do appreciate you coming by to tell me what happened, Cheryl."

"You're very welcome," she said and then paused. "But that is not exactly the only reason we're here."

Naomi had sat quietly up until now, but she eased forward on her seat and gave Cheryl an encouraging nod.

She swallowed nervously. "Mazee...how well did you say you knew my uncle Ralph?"

The question hung unanswered between them for several long seconds. Mazee's gaze darted from Cheryl to Naomi before falling to her hands, bunched tightly in her lap. Collecting herself, she laid one hand carefully over the other and sat up straight.

"How much do you know?"

So she wasn't going to deny that they'd been closer than she'd implied? Cheryl's chin rose. "I know you dated in high school. I know you apologized to him for something that happened before you graduated."

"Just after, actually," she said quietly. "We broke up not long after we graduated."

"Would you mind telling us why?" Naomi asked.

Mazee lifted her gaze, deep sorrow in the depths of her blue eyes. "I'm ashamed to admit that it was because I had fallen in love with someone else." She looked at Cheryl. "Your uncle realized it...probably before I did."

"Who was it?" Cheryl whispered, although she suspected she already knew. "Who did you fall in love with?"

Mazee's lips thinned, and her fine chin trembled. "Datschel Watters."

She rose abruptly, as if speaking his name made it unbearable to remain still. Her steps echoed against the wood floor as she began pacing the room. "We met while he was on his rumspringa.

At first I was just attracted to his straightforward way of looking at things. It was so different from anything else I knew. But then...it became something more, and Ralph..."

Her eyes shone with regret as she looked at Cheryl. "He seemed to sense when I lost my heart to Datschel. He bowed out like a true gentleman. No anger or recrimination. He simply wished me well, and that was that."

She reached to grasp one of Cheryl's hands earnestly. "I'm sorry I didn't tell you earlier. It was just so painful to think about and..."

She pulled away with a sigh. "I realize there is no way you could know Datschel or Trampas or any of the circumstances surrounding what happened, but I do." She frowned. "Although likely the way I remember it is very different from the account Jackson Mathers gave you. He told you about their rivalry, I suppose? And how competitive they could be?"

Cheryl's mouth dropped open. "He did, but how...?"

"How did I know you'd gone to see him?" She shook her head. "I didn't really. I guessed. After all, your interest in solving mysteries is no secret, and when you told me you'd stumbled on the articles, well, I figured it would be too much of a draw for you to ignore, especially when you learned that your uncle was involved."

"Plus I knew the reporter's name."

Mazee nodded. "That was how I knew your curiosity had been piqued." She sighed sadly and lifted her hand to smooth her hair behind her ear. "So? Am I right? Did Jackson tell you he suspected Datschel had something to do with his brother's death?"

Cheryl glanced at Naomi and then nodded slowly.

Mazee's jaw hardened. "That awful man. He was so arrogant... so certain he had all the answers..." She sputtered to a halt, her breathing heavy, and cast an apologetic glance at Naomi. "I'm sorry."

Naomi's hand fluttered in dismissal. "It is hard to keep unresolved feelings buried long."

"Unresolved?" Mazee gave a bitter laugh. "Yes, well, I suppose that would be one way to describe my attitude toward Jackson Mathers."

Her chest rose and fell rapidly, describing more aptly than words the agitation she felt inside. After a moment, she finally tamped her anger enough to speak.

"If you don't mind, I'd like to take a moment to tell you what really happened the night Trampas died. After that, you can decide for yourself if you believe Jackson's story or mine. Would that be all right?"

Mazee's grief, her hurt and anger, had a tangible effect on Cheryl. She reached out for Mazee but stopped shy of actually touching her, sensing that to do so would unleash a torrent of tears. "Of course, Mazee. If that's what you want," she encouraged gently.

Though she had offered, it took her some time to work up the courage to begin. With one hand, she gripped the arm of the chair so tightly, it turned her knuckles white, stirring compassion in Cheryl's heart, and Naomi's too, for she reached out to pat Mazee's shoulder.

"Datschel stopped by my house that night," she began quietly. "He told me his brother and father had fought, and he explained why. He said he was going out looking for Trampas. I can't explain what happened next except to say I had a bad feeling the moment he appeared on my doorstep. I asked him not to go. Begged really...I begged him not to go, but getting him to listen...he was so stubborn...it was like arguing with a post."

She seemed to realize she was stumbling over her words and drew a deep breath to steady herself before continuing. Her gaze dropped to her hands.

"Datschel told me about Trampas's dreams of becoming an Olympian. While he didn't understand them, he loved his brother and didn't want to lose him. He said he thought Trampas had gone to the river because that was where he'd first learned to swim. He insisted on going there to look for him."

She paused to wipe the tears from her eyes. "I wanted to go along, but Datschel refused. He was concerned about me...how it would look for us to be out alone together. He told me he would let me know once he'd found Trampas...once everything was settled. So I watched him leave and worried the whole time he was gone."

Naomi drew a tissue from a box next to the sofa and gave it to Mazee, who used it to swipe her nose and then folded it in her fingers. "Finally, I couldn't stand it any longer. I knew something was wrong. Datschel hadn't returned, hadn't called..." She lifted watery eyes to Cheryl. "It was so late, but I called the one person I knew I could trust, the one person I knew would help."

"Uncle Ralph."

She nodded.

"So *that's* how he knew where to go and why he arrived before the authorities."

"That's correct. Ralph was the one who called the police," Mazee said. "He went down to the river, just like he'd promised. He found Datschel holding Trampas…trying to do CPR…but it was too late."

Though she hated to interrupt, Cheryl couldn't stifle the question simmering on her tongue. "Mazee, I never really have understood…how is it that a swimmer as strong as Trampas…"

"How could he have drowned?"

Cheryl nodded, glad she'd understood and voiced the question for her.

Mazee sighed. "Datschel said he hit his head on a log. It knocked him unconscious. By the time Datschel got there, it was already too late, but he jumped in anyway, even though he wasn't nearly as strong a swimmer as his brother."

She leaned forward, her eyes suddenly piercing. "I know what Jackson told you, Cheryl. He said Datschel could have tried harder to pull Trampas from the river, but it's not true. Datschel did everything he could to save his brother. Ralph too. He wasn't trying to cover up what happened that night."

The last part caught Cheryl off guard. "You knew about that?"

She settled back against her chair. "Of course. Everyone knew what Jackson was accusing him of, but I was certain he could never be capable of such a thing. Ralph knew what would happen if the media learned of my relationship with Datschel. That's why he refused to say what he was doing there. He was trying to protect me…even after everything that had happened between us. Even after the rumors about Datschel and Trampas started and people began questioning Ralph's part, he stayed true. He'd made a promise to me not to say a word, and he kept that promise."

Silence followed while the three of them considered all that had been said. At last, Naomi spoke.

"It is all very sad, for sure and for certain." She shook her head and then looked at Mazee. "If I may?"

She nodded for her to continue.

"What about Datschel's father? How did he feel about a relationship between his son and...and an *Englischer*?"

Naomi wasn't looking at Cheryl, yet she sensed something unspoken in her words that made her stomach do a queer flip.

"Datschel never told his father about us," Mazee said, sparing Cheryl from pondering further. "But I never doubted his feelings for me. I knew the only thing keeping him from proposing was how his father would feel. Not that a relationship between us was forbidden," she added quickly. "Datschel had not yet taken his vows. He was just concerned for his father. I think he knew his brother was likely to leave the church and couldn't see hurting his father the same way. I think he feared it would be too much for him to bear."

"And..." Cheryl's mouth went dry. She swallowed and tried again. "And what about you? Did you ever consider becoming A-Amish?"

Mazee's eyes grew solemn. "I did. In fact, Datschel and I talked about it—argued really. I was ready to leave home, join the church...anything if it meant we could be together. But Datschel would not agree."

"What?" Cheryl and Naomi asked in unison.

"Why not?" Cheryl added. "Didn't he want you to join the church?"

Mazee lifted her hand. "No, no, it wasn't like that. He just knew what an enormous decision leaving my old life behind would be. He knew how much I loved my family, and he wanted me to be certain before I did something hasty. I told him I didn't want to wait, that I'd already made my decision, but he insisted, for my sake." She pressed her hand to her chest. "Still, I think knowing I would be willing to give up everything to be with him gave him reason to hope that we might have a future together. Gave us *both* reason to hope." Her shoulders drooped, and she looked suddenly very old and tired. "And then . . . in a heartbeat, everything changed. Trampas drowned and Datschel . . . "

Tears soaked her eyes. She took her time unfolding the tissue corner by corner and pressing it to her cheeks.

"Mazee, what happened to Datschel?" Naomi asked quietly.

The agonized reply seemed ripped from the very depths of her heart. "Datschel never got over his brother's death. His remorse drove him away from Sugarcreek, even after the police cleared him of wrongdoing."

But did that explain why Mazee had married elsewhere? How could she be sure Datschel wouldn't return? What would she have done if he had?

"I waited almost five years," she said, almost in answer to Cheryl's thoughts. "Waited and hoped that'd eventually I'd hear from him and he would explain where he'd gone or that he'd come back to Sugarcreek. He never did. And then I met Jonathan, and, well, after a while...I quit waiting."

"And you have no idea where he went?" Naomi pressed.

Mazee's face went strangely blank. Finally, she shook her head. "That man has lived with more crushing guilt and regret than anyone should ever have to bear. Wherever he is, I pray he's found a measure of peace. And that's also why"—her gaze drifted to Cheryl—"that's why I asked you to leave the past buried and why I must ask you again...please...focus on the more positive aspects of the town's history and leave the painful parts alone."

Cheryl's chest felt heavy, weighted. Though she understood Mazee's request, she still felt compelled to ask about the burned photos. "Mazee, can you think of anyone else in this town who might have wanted Datschel's past to stay buried?"

Her chin rose. "It could have been any number of people, I suppose. Not everyone believed in his guilt, you know. There were plenty of people who thought what happened was nothing more than a terribly unfortunate accident. Maybe somebody took it upon themselves to do what no one would all those years ago."

"And what was that?" Cheryl asked.

"The right thing," Mazee insisted firmly. "Maybe they were just trying to do the right thing."

While it wasn't exactly a satisfactory answer, it was, Cheryl knew, the only one she was likely to get. She thanked Mazee for her time, and then she and Naomi excused themselves and left.

An uneasy silence filled the car on the way home. Cheryl was glad to learn the details of her uncle's involvement with the Watters brothers, but hearing about Mazee and Datschel's doomed love filled her with sorrow.

"You are very quiet," Naomi said at last, her voice only slightly louder than the hum of engine and rumble of the tires.

Cheryl heaved a sigh. "I just can't help thinking about Mazee and Datschel, and how different her life would have been had they ended up together."

Naomi pondered this a moment. "Different? Ja, I daresay that is correct. But better?" She shook her head. "Not necessarily."

Cheryl took her eyes off the road long enough to shoot a quick glance at her. "What do you mean?"

She clutched the seat belt at her shoulder, her voice low but steady and filled with confidence. "Gott has a way of working all things for our goot, ain't so? Could be that things happened exactly the way they did because He had a bigger plan."

"Like what?" Cheryl asked, doubtfully. While she knew what the Scriptures had to say about God's provision, convincing her heart was much more difficult.

"Well, I noticed several photographs back there, in Mazee's home. I assume they were her grandchildren?"

"Probably," Cheryl said. "I've heard her mention them once or twice."

"And she teaches Bible study at your church, ain't so?"

"True," Cheryl agreed. "But what does that have to do with God having a bigger plan?"

Naomi tapped her kapp. "I just think that though her life is not what Mazee expected, much goot has come of it."

Cheryl pondered this silently. It was true that Mazee's children might never have been born had she not married Jonathan. One of them was a doctor who specialized in cancer research. How many lives had been affected just by his birth? And her daughter had four children of her own. What might have become of them had things been different?

After a moment, she said, "So why do you think God allowed Datschel and Mazee to fall in love in the first place? I mean, if they were never meant to be together, why didn't He keep them from caring about one another?"

"That I do not know," Naomi answered softly. "I suppose there are many of Gotte's ways that will remain a mystery while we are on this side of heaven, but I trust that one day He will reveal His purpose to them. Until then?" She shrugged and shifted on the seat to look at Cheryl. "And speaking of mysteries, we still do not have an answer about your photographs."

"I know." Frustration roiled in her belly. "I mean, who do we know who might have had a reason to destroy those things?"

She mentally ran through the list of people in any way attached to the Watters case. Suddenly, a name popped into her head—one she'd not considered.

"Violet!"

Naomi jumped, and she grabbed for the dash.

"Sorry. Didn't mean to scare you." Cheryl slowed the car as she allowed her suspicions to take shape. "It has to be Violet, Naomi. I don't know why I didn't think of her before."

Naomi's face showed her doubt. "She *is* Datschel's sister, but to go into a church and set fire to your things... it does not fit with the image of the woman I know. Besides, we have not even considered the possibility of it being someone else."

"That's true, but remember, Violet did try to keep from answering my questions at the library," Cheryl insisted. "Plus, she knew exactly what material I found and what I planned to do with it." She held up two fingers. "In other words, she had the knowledge and the motive. As for the opportunity, well, that could have been purely chance."

Even as Cheryl attempted to explain, Naomi shook her head stubbornly.

"Ne. I do not like jumping to conclusions without giving Violet the chance to explain. We should talk to her, face-to-face, after we have taken some time to think on the things we learned. Tomorrow, if we still believe Violet was involved, we will go to see her. And if she says she does not know what happened, we will take her at her word. Agreed?"

Much as Cheryl hated to admit it, Naomi was right. Jumping to conclusions had never gotten anyone very far, and it wouldn't do for them to start now.

"Agreed," she said, reluctantly, and then more brightly, "So I'll pick you up tomorrow?"

"Tomorrow?"

"So we can go over the list of suspects... I mean the list of people who may have been involved."

Naomi caught her attempt at humor and grinned. "Ja, you can pick me up tomorrow. Come at noon. I will have lunch ready."

"Sounds good. And then we'll go to see Violet?"

"Maybe."

"All right, maybe."

Cheryl pressed on the accelerator. Outwardly, she pretended to have laid her suspicions about Violet to rest, but in her head, she was already planning what she would say.

Chapter Seventeen

The inviting scent of fresh bread greeted Cheryl the moment she walked into the Millers' house the next day. Seth and Levi and the rest of the Miller clan had eaten and were already on their way out when she arrived, but she was glad for a glimpse of Levi as she made her way to the kitchen. Their gazes held for a moment longer than necessary, and it seemed he saved his smile for her alone. Oh, but keeping her promise not to act on her feelings was proving difficult!

Blowing out a steadying breath, she stepped into the kitchen, where Naomi had two plates with thick turkey sandwiches on homemade bread waiting.

"Sorry I'm late." Cheryl laid her coat and scarf over a chair and went to the counter to pour two glasses of lemonade from a pitcher. "Things got really busy right before lunch, so I waited to leave until they'd settled down some."

Naomi waved dismissively and carried the plates to the table. "That is no problem. With everyone out of the house, we should have plenty of time to talk."

Hearing Naomi use such casual speech drew a smile as Cheryl set the lemonade alongside the sandwiches. They paused for a moment of silent prayer before digging in to the food.

"So have you had time to think about everything that happened yesterday?" Naomi asked. She pulled a napkin from a basket on the table and handed it to Cheryl then took one for herself.

Cheryl nodded and used the napkin to wipe the crumbs from her fingers. "I have to admit, things looked a little different this morning after a good night's sleep." She lifted her palm before Naomi could jump in with praise. "Now, I still think Violet knows more than she's saying, but I have to agree that there are plenty of other people who may have had reason to keep things hushed."

Naomi swallowed a bite of her sandwich, her eyes wide. "Such as?"

"Jackson Mathers, for one." Cheryl leaned forward. "He all but accused my uncle of wrongdoing. If he knew everything he said all those years ago was incorrect, or even an outright lie, wouldn't he want to cover it up?"

Naomi nodded, her fingers plucking absently at her napkin. "Ja, that makes goot sense."

"And what about Muddy?"

"Muddy?" Naomi drew back, a look of puzzlement on her face. "I do not understand. Was he not the one who put out the fire?"

"Yes, but only after I called for help," Cheryl reminded her. "Who's to say it wasn't him who started the fire in the first place?"

"Why would he do that?"

Cheryl frowned and picked up her sandwich. "Well, I didn't say I had all the answers."

They laughed and spent a few moments savoring their food. Naomi took a sip of her lemonade and then set aside her glass.

"Well, one thing is certain, I agree that we should probably still talk to Violet, if for no other reason than to let her know what has happened. I think we owe her that much. It does involve her family after all."

The decision made, Cheryl could hardly finish her sandwich fast enough. With the dishes washed and put away and the kitchen once again put in order, she and Naomi climbed into her car and made a beeline for the library. There, Cheryl was disappointed to learn that Violet had requested the day off and would most likely be found at home. Fortunately, that wasn't far, and they pulled into the driveway a short while later.

"Naomi, wait." Cheryl laid her hand on Naomi's arm, stopping her as she reached for the door handle.

She raised her eyebrows. "Is something wrong?"

Cheryl looked at the house, studying it as though seeing it for the first time. Inside was a family with hurts long buried. Were they right digging up all that pain anew? Couldn't she just accept that her uncle had helped a friend in need?

Naomi leaned across the seat, closing the gap between them. "You were right yesterday, when you said we owed it to her. Maybe knowing there are others who believe in her bruder's innocence and who would go to such lengths to protect him will help loosen some of her guilt that has burrowed in so deep."

"If it wasn't her, you mean? If it wasn't her who burned the photographs? Or Jackson? Who maybe did it simply to protect himself even at the expense of my uncle's reputation?"

Cheryl's words carried an edge of anger she couldn't begin to understand—not without looking deep inside. She reached for the handle instead.

"All right then. Let's go talk to Violet."

Empathy flickered in Naomi's eyes, but she said nothing as they made their way up the path to the door. Once again she knocked, and a short time later Violet answered. Spying them on the porch, she wiped her hands on the apron she wore over her plain dress and beckoned them inside. A crackling fire burned in the fireplace, inviting them to slip out of their heavy coats. Violet laid their garments on a bench in the hall before leading them to a sofa and chairs facing the fire.

She licked her lips and wrung her hands nervously. Her gaze flitted from Naomi to Cheryl. "I assume this visit is in regard to my bruder?"

"In a way," Cheryl said. Though tempted to skim over the details and jump to the question burning in her head, she resisted. Starting with their last visit, she informed Violet of everything they'd discovered and all that had happened since. When she got to the part about the fire at the church, she slowed to study Violet's reaction.

"By the time we discovered where the smoke was coming from, it was too late," she finished. "Everything was destroyed, including the articles I collected from the library and the photos given to me by Mazee Stillwell."

Behind her thick glasses, Violet's eyes widened. "But why would anyone do such a terrible thing? What if the fire had spread and someone had gotten hurt? Besides, surely they realized how easy it would be for you to reprint the things you found. Why bother destroying them?"

"Perhaps it was a warning?" Naomi said. "A not-so-subtle way of telling us to leave the past in the past? Or perhaps it was much more innocent, and whoever burned those things was simply trying to protect Datschel."

Violet's gaze jumped to Naomi and back. "Protect..." Her cheeks reddened, and her voice turned strident. "You think I did this?" She stiffened as she spoke, until she sat impossibly straight and still.

"We don't know," Cheryl said, answering honestly. "But if you didn't, we felt we owed it to you to let you know what happened."

"But...but why blame me? What have I done that would make you think me capable of such a crime?"

"It's what you didn't do." Cheryl spread her hands in silent appeal. "You said it yourself—you regretted not sticking up for your brother when you had the chance."

Her face flushed, but she nodded. "Ja. I did say that, and I do regret what happened all those years ago, but burning your things? This I did not do."

There was a moment of quiet, and then Naomi gave a curt nod. "Then we must try to find out who did, ain't so? And what compelled them, before anything else happens."

Violet seemed genuinely relieved by her response and let out a long breath. "I cannot answer the *who*, but perhaps we can figure out the *why*." She turned to look at Cheryl. "The things that were burned, you said it was the articles from the library, ja?"

Cheryl nodded. "Among other things. There was also a large envelope with old photos of the town, some maps, a few railroad plans, things like that."

Violet stopped her with an upraised hand. "Tell me more about the articles. There was more than one?"

"Oh yes, there were several. I went back as far as the night the accident happened and printed everything I could find."

Violet pinched her bottom lip. "Ach, I wish we were at the library now. I would like to see those articles again for myself." Her hand fell. "I do not suppose you can tell me what was in them?"

"Some," Cheryl said hesitantly. One part in particular was burned into her memory. She relayed what she could remember, and when she reached the part pertaining to Uncle Ralph, she hesitated. "The...um...the article said Uncle Ralph was one of the first on the scene and questioned his motives in stepping in to keep Datschel from speaking to police until his attorney arrived."

Violet gave a slow nod. "So this is why you set off in search of more information?"

Cheryl's face warmed. "Partly, yes."

She wasn't certain if Violet knew of her brother's affection for Mazee, but if not, she didn't want to be the one to spill Mazee's secret.

She went on with a wave. "Anyway, it was enough to push me into searching for the person who wrote the article, a man by the name of..."

"Jackson Mathers. I remember." Her lips pursed, forming tiny wrinkles around her mouth.

Cheryl exchanged a glance with Naomi. Apparently, she did not remember him kindly. She cleared her throat. "I went to see him a few days ago. He lives in an assisted living facility outside of New Philadelphia."

The tension eased from Violet's features. "I wondered what became of him after he wrote that story. I never did believe his version of what happened, even after Datschel disappeared and the rumors started circulating."

Cheryl leaned forward in almost the same moment as Naomi. "His version? You mean to say you think he made it up? But why would he do that? What reason could he have?"

Violet's face registered surprise. "You mean you do not know?"

Naomi broke the shocked silence. "Perhaps you should explain."

She hesitated a moment, her eyes troubled behind the thick glasses. Apparently, whatever she needed to say still bothered her, even after all this time.

"Jackson Mathers's account was biased by something that happened many years ago," Violet stated, hesitantly at first and then more matter-of-factly. "Long before your aunt Mitzi came to Sugarcreek." She tilted her head, thinking. "Before you came too, Naomi, come to think of it." She gave a curt nod. "Regardless, Jackson Mathers's vendetta had less to do with Datschel and Trampas and more to do with our father."

"Your father?" Naomi exclaimed, robbing the words off Cheryl's tongue. This was most definitely a turn neither of them had seen coming. "What do you mean?"

Violet grasped her glasses and adjusted the frames, her wide eyes solemn behind the thick lenses. "You see, many years ago, Jackson used to be a pretty well-known reporter. His father owned one of the largest newspapers in Tuscarawas County, but he was not a very good businessman."

She directed a glance at Naomi. "It is not gossip to tell you such things?" Though she appeared confident, her tone held a note of question.

Naomi encouraged her with a shake of her head. "We will take care not to discuss the flaws of others."

Violet agreed with a solemn nod. "As we learned later," she continued, "the only thing keeping him afloat was the war."

She frowned and bumped her palm against her forehead. "Ach, that did not come out quite right. What I meant to say was that people were interested in any reports they could find on the progress of the war. When it ended, the paper began losing money, and before too long he was forced to sell. Only there were not too many buyers for failing newspapers."

"Let me guess," Cheryl said. "The man who bought the paper was your father?"

She nodded. "He did not keep it long. It passed from his hands to another after only a few years. I think you would probably recognize the name. Years ago, it used to be called the *Sugarcreek Budget*."

"You mean *The Budget*? Our Amish newspaper?" Naomi exclaimed.

Violet chuckled. "The very same."

Both Cheryl and Naomi fell silent as they let the information sink in.

Finally, Cheryl shook her head. "There's something I don't understand. If your father kept the paper running, why didn't Jackson just go to work for him?"

Violet tsked sadly. "Jackson felt his father sold too low. He claimed that my father took advantage of his situation. He resented the Amish—all Amish—for many years after the paper sold."

"And so he went to work for another paper, only there he didn't have his father's name to give him a leg up. He was a lowly reporter. Nothing more."

Violet said nothing, but behind her glasses, her deep brown eyes appeared troubled. After a moment, Cheryl rose and Naomi with her.

Cheryl eased around the couch and crossed to take Violet's hand. "Well, I suppose we had better be going. Thank you very much for your time, Violet."

Violet stood to accept Cheryl's outstretched hand, but held on longer than necessary. "I am very glad I could help. If you hear anything...or...if you..."

She stopped, her breathing flustered.

"I will let you know," Cheryl assured quietly.

She stepped back as Naomi bent her head close to whisper something encouraging in Pennsylvania Dutch. Cheryl couldn't help but be envious. Though they weren't related, the two shared a language and a kinship that sprang from a common faith. Would she ever be able to say the same?

They said their good-byes to Violet, and then Cheryl drove Naomi home. Though she invited her to stay, Cheryl didn't take her up on the offer, choosing instead to return to Sugarcreek so she could close up the Swiss Miss before popping into the library to do a little more investigating into Jackson Mathers's past.

It was after five by the time she arrived at the library, but that meant most of the other patrons had gone home and Cheryl had the computers to herself. She began online first, but when nearly an hour of searching led nowhere, she turned to the microfiche. Once again, she found herself searching through rolls of film, reading until the words began to blur and her eyes hurt. Finally, she pressed her fingers to her temple in a vain attempt to rub away the beginning of a headache.

"No luck, huh? Something I can help you find?"

At the sound of Pam's voice, Cheryl opened her eyes and sat back in her chair. "You saw that, huh?"

Pam smiled. "You looked like you might be a little frustrated. Looking for anything in particular?"

"I am, actually." She didn't go into much detail, but Cheryl did give her the gist of what she hoped to find and why.

"Mathers. Mathers." Pam tapped her fingernail against the side of the microfiche reader. "Seems like I remember that name." She snapped her fingers. "I know ... he used to own the newspaper ... the Amish one."

"*The Budget.*"

"That's it. But he sold it years ago."

Cheryl nodded. "That's correct. Any idea why?"

She frowned, thinking. "Goodness, no. That was a long time ago. I have no idea."

Cheryl sighed. "Well, I heard it was due to some business troubles, but I haven't been able to find anything to corroborate that information."

"Were you looking under his company name?" Pam asked, her eyebrows raised innocently.

"C-company name?" Suddenly, Cheryl had the urge to smack herself on the forehead.

"Yeah. Creston Media, I think." She placed her hands on her hips. "Or something like that. He named it after his wife. Her last name was Creston." She widened her eyes and tilted her head. "Very wealthy family. Like Rockefeller wealthy."

"Any idea what kind of business they were in? How did they make their money?"

She shrugged. "What else? Steel. Her father owned one of the largest steel companies in Ohio."

"Great. Thank you. I'll check it out."

Cheryl hurried back to the computers. And because the headlines had made national news, it wasn't difficult to pull up information on the once lucrative publishing giant. She settled into her chair with a sigh of relief knowing she wouldn't have to resort to sorting through more microfilm. Or at least, not much more. If necessary, she could use the dates on the information she found online to narrow her search on film.

In the end, she didn't have to.

Much had been written regarding the steady decline of Creston Media, but not because of Jackson Mathers or his father, Preston. As Pam had said, his wife, Delia, had come from wealth, and the money Preston had used to build Creston Media belonged to her. When he lost it, the headlines hinted at marital troubles, all of which ended when she died of cancer and he sold the paper.

Or...did they?

Two words jumped at Cheryl from the narrative description of one particular Web site in her Google search—legal woes. Obviously, Preston Mathers would have had "legal woes" if he'd been forced to sell, yet something drew her attention, prompting her to read further. She clicked the link and scrolled through the archived pages until she found the one she sought.

"'Creston Media founder facing legal battle,'" she read out loud. The article went on to describe investigations, which led to hearings, which led to criminal charges, many of which dragged on long after the publishing company closed its doors.

Cheryl bit her lip, thinking. Could it be that Preston Mathers had sold his newspaper not because it was losing money...but to pay his legal fees? Once his wife died, the Creston family *could* have cut him off, especially if he'd already spent all of his wife's money. Insurance policy? Certainly they'd had one. Where had all that money gone?

Suspicion rooted in Cheryl's thoughts. She grabbed an old cashier register receipt from a pocket of her purse and scribbled down several dates. If she did have to come back for more research on the microfiche, she didn't want to have to start from the beginning. Gathering up her things, she debated calling Naomi and then decided speaking to her in person was better. She waved good-bye to Pam and headed out the door, her keys in hand.

But just outside of Sugarcreek, she spotted a familiar figure in a long black coat ambling along the highway. She slowed to go around him. Sure enough, it was Muddy. His collar was turned up, and he walked with his head down. Somewhere along the way, he'd picked up a pair of bright yellow work gloves, and he clutched a bulky grocery sack. Cheryl couldn't help but wonder where he was headed on such a cold evening. He didn't look up as she passed, and for a long time, she watched him in the rearview mirror while a small voice inside spoke quietly to her heart.

She should stop.

She should see where he was going.

She should see if she could help.

She wasn't in the habit of picking up hitchhikers, but Muddy wasn't hitching a ride, and he wasn't a stranger. Exactly. And she didn't like the way things had ended the last time she saw him, so if she didn't want to feel that same unease...

Sighing, she pulled over on to the shoulder and then put the car in reverse. When she reached him, she lowered the window and leaned out. "Muddy?"

Snowflakes dotted his head and shoulders as he bent toward her window. "Miss Cooper?"

"Hi, Muddy." She reached over and shut off the radio. "It's getting late, and the weather is supposed to turn bad later tonight. Can I give you a lift somewhere?"

He shook his head quickly. "Oh no, Miss Cooper. That won't be necessary. I can walk."

"But"—she scanned the dark road ahead—"you're headed out of town."

"Yes, ma'am. I'm hoping to get to New Philadelphia tonight."

"Muddy, that's over ten miles away! It'll take you hours to get there." She glanced at her watch, calculating the time it would take him to get there and figuring it would take most of the night, even at a brisk pace.

His mouth curved in a lopsided grin. "Walking keeps me warm." He straightened. "Well, I'd best get moving."

He took several steps. Cheryl pulled even with him. She could not in good conscience let him go that far alone, at night, with the snow making it difficult for drivers to see. What if he got hit?

She leaned sideways and called out the window again. "Muddy, please, I really wouldn't mind taking you, and...I'd feel better if you let me give you a lift."

He hesitated and looked down the road in the direction from which he'd come.

"Really, Muddy, I don't mind," Cheryl urged. She patted the passenger seat. "Please."

"Well, it is a pretty long walk. If you're sure?" He hitched the bag on to his hip.

"Of course. Climb in."

She hit the Unlock button and waited while he circled the car.

"Push that seat back," Cheryl instructed after Muddy opened the door. "It's the little lever on the side."

He slid the seat back as far as it would go. His height made her Ford Focus seem even smaller than normal, but he didn't complain as he dropped his grocery sack into the backseat and then folded himself into the car. He pulled the seat belt across his chest and snapped it into place while Cheryl adjusted the heating vents to blow in his direction.

"Thank you, Miss Cooper," he said, tugging off his gloves to blow on his hands. "I confess, I wasn't looking forward to a chilly walk, but I really do need to get to New Philadelphia tonight."

"But, Muddy, it's so late. Why didn't you wait until morning?"

"It just couldn't wait."

He refused to say more, and Cheryl didn't press. "Well, I'm glad I happened to drive by. And by the way, call me Cheryl."

He nodded but wouldn't look at her. It was surprising, really, how little she knew about Muddy, she thought as she pulled back out on to the road. She had no idea what he did with his time or where he spent his days.

She cleared her throat nervously. "So, um, have you eaten? We can stop for a hamburger on the way if you want."

"Oh, no thank you, Miss—I mean, Cheryl." He looked uncomfortable saying her name, yet he managed it and went on. "I can grab something at the shelter."

"Is that where you were headed? A shelter in New Philadelphia?"

He nodded. "Bethel Outreach Center. It's off of Union Avenue."

So that was where he slept. She typed the name into her phone and waited while the navigation called it up. In a few minutes, she was pulling up to a single-story brick building with bright green shutters and a sign above the door that read, Come to Me all you who are weary...

"This looks like a nice place," she said as she slipped the car into Park. She craned her neck to peer out of the windshield. There were lights in many of the windows but through the largest one, she could see people moving back and forth carrying plates of food and cups. "Looks like it might be suppertime."

Gladness filled her that even though he hadn't accepted her offer to stop for food, he would be getting a warm meal.

"Yes, ma'am, it sure does." He lowered his gaze, and redness colored his cheeks. "Well, I'd better get inside. Thank you very much for the ride."

He reached for the door handle and started to climb out.

"Muddy, wait." Cheryl reached into the backseat. "Don't forget your..."

She'd been about to say "clothes," but the grocery sack felt much too heavy to contain an extra pair of pants.

"Oh yes. Thank you. I'll get it." He opened the back door, and when he grabbed the sack, she heard the distinctive clink of cans. He smiled as he closed the door and pressed the sack close. "Looks like I made it in time after all."

"In time?"

He nodded. "To bring these canned goods for the meal."

"Wait…" Shame filled her for the conclusions she'd drawn. "You mean you came to *help* with the meal?"

He looked confused as he glanced down at the bag and back. "Well…yes. I can't get here every week, but I try to make it when I can." Suddenly, his face went blank, and his jaw hardened. "Oh, I see." He stepped back from the car, and his grip on the grocery sack tightened, crumpling the paper. "I didn't steal this food, Miss Cooper. I used some of the money I got from the church to pay for it, only it came later than normal, which is why you found me walking when you did."

Cheryl shook her head. "No, Muddy, I didn't mean…"

She stumbled to a stop. Her real meaning wasn't much better than his misplaced assumption. Still, she couldn't leave him believing that she thought him a thief. She eased sideways on the seat, angling her head to peer out the passenger window. "I know you didn't steal that food, Muddy. I'm just ashamed that it didn't occur to me that you would be coming to the shelter to help others. I'm sorry."

His grip on the sack slowly lessened until at last he quit from clutching it and held it at his side. "No need to apologize. I suppose I might have made the same conclusion had I been in your seat." He smiled—a genuine one that reached his eyes. "Thank you again for the ride."

"You're welcome. I'm glad I could help."

He pushed the passenger door half-closed then stopped and pulled it open again.

"You be careful driving home, okay, Cheryl? The roads are likely to get slippery the later it gets."

"I will. Thank you, Muddy."

He gave one last nod in her direction before closing the door and turning to make his way inside. Though there was no reason to stay, it was several minutes before Cheryl could bring herself to drive away, and her thoughts kept her occupied most of the way home. Without realizing it, she'd formed misconceptions about Muddy—who he was and why he was in his current state. Perhaps she would do well to follow his example and volunteer in a homeless shelter from time to time.

It was this thought that accompanied her as she climbed into bed later that night, with Beau curled on to the pillow next to her head. People weren't always what they seemed. She'd learned that watching Muddy today. Mostly, people were just trying to get along, but once in a while...

Once in a while, they really could surprise you.

CHAPTER EIGHTEEN

Cheryl looked up from the customer she was helping when the bell above the door to the Swiss Miss chimed and Levi walked in. Even bundled in his heavy coat, she couldn't help but admire the way he looked silhouetted against the bright light streaming from the windows. He was broad shouldered and sturdy and completely unaware of the way women stopped to watch him as he passed.

"Uh, so anyway," she stammered, turning her attention back to the elderly woman holding Amish dolls in both hands, "if you decide you'd like to order a few more of these, just let me know and I'll take down your information."

The woman nodded, thanked her, and went back to browsing. Cheryl made her way to the counter where Levi waited. Inside, her stomach fluttered nervously.

"Good morning. You're in town early today. Everything okay at the farm?"

Levi looked surprisingly uncomfortable standing there with his hands shoved into his pockets. "Everything is fine. I just had some time so . . . we needed some supplies from the lumber store, and I figured I would head into town while I was waiting for Larry to fill the order."

So he hadn't come specifically to see her. She crammed a lid on to her disappointment and forced a smile. "I see. Well, I'm glad you stopped by."

Lame, but under the circumstances, it was the best she could manage. She mimicked his stance and shoved her hands into her pockets. "Say, if you talk to Naomi later..."

If he talked to her? Of course he would. She resisted the urge to face-palm.

"Anyway, would you let her know we're running low on cheese?"

"Of course."

Sugar and grits. Now the only thing they could find to talk about was cheese? What happened to their agreement to remain friends? Warmth built in her chest and pressed up, up. She could feel it rising to her neck. Soon, there would be no hiding it.

"Well, I suppose I had better get back to work. See you later, Levi."

She didn't wait for his response and had half turned to move away when his touch on her arm pulled her back.

"Cheryl, wait. I was wondering...if you are not busy later...I mean if you have not already made plans...I thought maybe you would like to get some lunch."

It was strange, seeing the normally stalwart Levi blushing and fumbling for words. Though tempted by the offer, Cheryl found herself hesitating. Pizza between friends was one thing, but this felt much more personal. More like dating. More like dangerous.

She tossed a quick glance about the store and then licked her lips nervously. "I...uh...that is...I don't have any plans, but..." Her chest tightened as she lowered her voice and forced the words out. "We've already gone out to eat together once this week. I thought we agreed we wouldn't try to pursue a relationship."

He fidgeted with the buttons on his coat. "That is true but..."

"But?"

But...she didn't want to risk her heart or their friendship.

After a moment, he stopped fidgeting to look her squarely in the eyes. "What is the saying you *Englisch* have? That does not mean we cannot be friends? And friends have to eat, ja?"

His attempt at humor only slightly relieved the ache that settled deep in her heart. "No, Levi. I mean, yes, friends have to eat, but *this* isn't that. There's no reason for us..."

"You want a reason?" He cocked his head as though thinking and rubbing his chin between thumb and forefinger. "How about this? We have not talked about the history project I was supposed to be helping you with."

"Levi..."

"All right then, what about this? I talked to Daed about the Watters brothers. He does remember something."

Her curiosity piqued, Cheryl studied him through narrowed eyelids. "*Hmm*...funny that you are just now mentioning that little fact."

He grinned. "So? Lunch?"

She planted her hands on her hips and lifted her chin. "All right. I get off at noon, when Esther comes in."

"I will meet you here. We can walk to Yoder's."

She shook her head. "No need. I can just meet you there."

A strange look of longing flitted across his face that made her regret the hasty words. It wasn't his fault, after all, that they were so different. They had both agreed to set their feelings aside rather than risk their hearts on something that had no hope.

"On second thought, why don't you stop by?" she offered cautiously and then berated herself for the joy she felt upon seeing the smile that blossomed on his face. Levi would not be the one who had his heart broken in this situation. He would be true to their vow to remain distant. Friends. While she on the other hand would likely fall head over heels and have her heart crushed to smithereens.

Still, she couldn't help but keep one eye on the time. As the morning wore on, she felt excitement build in her chest until she forgot all about Jackson or his father or even Uncle Ralph. What mattered was spending time with Levi and pretending, even if just for an afternoon, that all was right between them.

When Esther arrived, Cheryl hurried to the back for a quick check of her hair and makeup before grabbing her coat and meeting Levi at the door.

"I'll be back soon, Esther," she called, blushing at the knowing glance the young girl flashed their way.

"Take your time." Esther offered a lighthearted wave. "I can take care of things here."

There was little doubt about the idea she had in her head, but rather than set her straight, Cheryl stepped outside and waited for Levi to join her.

Together, they turned up the street toward Yoder's Corner.

"Did you get everything you needed from Weaver's?" Cheryl asked, anxious to fill the silence with small talk rather than risk having the conversation run toward more serious matters.

Up and down the street, people were hurrying in and out of shops, most laden with packages and bags in preparation for Thanksgiving. Shocked to realize that she'd let several days slip by, Cheryl made a mental note to add a trip to the grocery store to her to-do list.

"Ja, we got everything. Daed will be pleased that we can get on with the repairs to the barn now. He was hoping to have it all finished before the bad weather really sets in."

And now... the weather. Sorrow pressed on Cheryl's heart. She missed the closeness she and Levi had shared, but to dwell on it would only make her sad. She forced a smile and listened while he outlined the plans for the barn and the corral beyond. By the time they reached Yoder's, she even felt a bit of the old companionship returning. Maybe this whole "friendship" thing wouldn't be so bad. Maybe they *could* see each other from time to time without it turning into anything more.

"Levi!"

Both she and Levi turned toward the bright voice calling to them from across the street. An Amish girl Cheryl did not recognize hurried toward them, a smile fixed to her pretty face and her shining eyes fixed... somewhere else.

Cheryl gulped back a sudden swell of fear. Who was this young woman, and why was she staring so possessively at Levi? Worse yet, why was he suddenly avoiding Cheryl's gaze?

The girl slid to a stop and stared expectantly up at Levi. Though it took some time, he managed a low, "Hello, Ellen."

"Have you heard?"

Rather than answer her question, he held his hand toward Cheryl. "Ellen, have you met Cheryl Cooper? She is the proprietor of the Swiss Miss."

Ellen's gaze swung to rest on Cheryl only briefly. She mumbled a polite hello and then turned back to Levi. "Well?"

Levi cleared his throat. "Ja, Ellen, I have heard."

"Heard what?" Even to her own ears, Cheryl's voice sounded choked.

Ellen turned up her pert nose—a move Cheryl had seen many an English girl practice. When she didn't answer, Levi was forced to respond.

"Ellen is from my district. "

"I have decided to join the church," she offered at last, a hint of triumph in her voice where there should have been only humble joy. "And after I make my vows, I will settle down and start a family."

"Ellen," Levi chided gently but not before Cheryl had gotten her full gist. This girl had set her kapp for Levi, and by the look of him, he was well aware of that fact.

Cheryl crossed her arms defensively over her heart.

"Maam and Daed are across the street," Ellen continued, obviously unaffected by his quiet reprimand. "Will you come to say hello?"

Levi shot a rather embarrassed glance at Cheryl. "I am sorry, Ellen. I am afraid I cannot today. Please give them my regards."

Though he refused her invitation, he didn't explain why he couldn't go, Cheryl noted. Suddenly, her stomach felt full of lead. Ellen said something in Pennsylvania Dutch. Levi responded in kind, and while Cheryl couldn't understand either of them, it was obvious by the glower that fell over Ellen's features that she wasn't happy.

Levi started to say more, but Cheryl stopped him with a light touch on his arm.

"You know, I really wouldn't mind if you wanted to go and say hello to Ellen's parents."

Levi tore his gaze from Ellen to look at Cheryl. "What about your lunch?"

Cheryl's heart plummeted. That was all he was worried about? Somehow she managed a casual shrug. "I can grab something to go. It's not a problem, really. I have a lot to do at the store today anyway."

"Goot." Ellen clasped her hands together. "Then you *can* come. I will go and tell them. They will be glad to see you." She turned to Cheryl. "It was nice to meet you, Miss Cooper."

At least she had some manners, Cheryl thought, bristling as the girl hurried back the way she'd come.

"I am sorry, Cheryl..."

"Don't worry about it," she replied curtly, before he could finish. "I'll see you later."

Levi shook his head adamantly. "Ne. You must let me explain before you go."

"That really isn't necessary," she said, though deep inside, it wasn't true. She wanted an explanation, wanted him to tell her that while Ellen obviously had ideas, he did not reciprocate them.

"I want to," he said, his voice firm and free of the uncertainty Cheryl felt inside.

Secretly, she was glad he insisted. She nodded for him to continue.

"Ellen is young. Sometimes her exuberance gets the best of her, but she is kind and generous, and she will make a goot addition to the church."

"Okay," she said slowly. When was he going to get to the part about her misplaced ideas about them?

"Listen, Cheryl, I am very sorry. I really did want to speak to her father, but I can do it another time if...?"

He *wanted* to speak to Ellen's father? Suddenly, Cheryl's face felt hot and her palms were sweating. "No...don't worry. It's fine, actually. Like I said, things were pretty busy at the store this morning, so it probably would be best if I got back to help Esther."

He hesitated. "Are you certain?"

"Of course." She said it with so much confidence, she almost convinced herself. "I don't mind at all."

He smiled, and this time he looked almost eagerly back the way Ellen had gone. "Okay, then. Danki, Cheryl. I will see you later?"

"Yep. Later. Tell Naomi hello for me," she called, but it was already too late.

Levi was headed across the street, and he was taking all of her misplaced hopes with him.

CHAPTER NINETEEN

Determined not to dwell on Levi, or allow her thoughts to linger on why he wanted to speak to Ellen's father, Cheryl spent the rest of the afternoon cozying up the store for Thanksgiving. Bright flowers made colorful displays in the windows and on the shelves, and where she could, she placed fragrant pumpkins and knobby squash. Cinnamon sticks and scented candles added a festive aroma, but even these could not completely erase the disappointment from Cheryl's heart. At a quarter to five, she checked out the last customer and decided to close early.

She had just finished counting out the money from the cash register when a knock on the door caught her attention. Naomi stood outside, her hand shielding her eyes as she peered through the window.

"Coming!" Cheryl slid the money and receipts into a bank bag then hurried to the door to let Naomi in. The temperature had begun to fall, and Naomi entered on a gust of frigid air, her cloak flapping like wings around her legs.

"Come in," Cheryl urged, certain her friend had to be chilled to the bone. "It's freezing outside. What are you doing in town so late?"

Naomi puffed heavily as she unwound a blue knit scarf from around her neck. "It is colder today, for sure and for certain."

"Is everything all right at the farm?"

Naomi gave a quick nod and rubbed her hands briskly over her arms. "Everything is fine. It is just that we have not spoken since we left Violet's house. You have been on my mind today, and well..." She narrowed her eyes to peer at Cheryl. "Something told me I should check on you."

Instantly, her eyes began to burn. "Oh. Thank you, Naomi. That's just...really sweet." The last word ended on a choked sort of half sob that rose up quickly in her throat.

Naomi pulled a handkerchief from her sleeve and gave it to Cheryl. "Ach, I thought something was wrong. Come. I had better fix us both some tea while you tell me all about it."

Thankful for her no-nonsense manner, Cheryl followed as Naomi led the way to her office.

"So? Have you done any more research into the town history project?" Naomi spared her a quick glance and then took the box of tea from the filing cabinet. She selected a bag of chamomile and held the box for Cheryl.

She plucked a bag of cinnamon and apple from the box and laid it on the desk. "I'm afraid not," she admitted guiltily. "I've been so wrapped up with Uncle Ralph, I've kinda let the history project slide. If I don't get around to it soon, I may have to talk to Dwight and Suzy about finding someone else to do it."

Naomi shrugged as she filled two mugs with water. "Did they say it had to be completed by a certain time?"

She sighed. "Not exactly, but I really don't want to procrastinate and risk leaving them in a lurch."

Naomi set the mugs in the microwave and set the timer. "The festival is not for another year, ain't so? You have plenty of time between now and then to get it finished."

"I suppose." Cheryl nibbled a corner of her fingernail and then, reminded of her mother's teaching on the habit, rested her hands in her lap.

"I saw Levi today," she offered tentatively, unsure of how much to say, but eager for a friend to share her thoughts.

"He stopped by?"

The timer dinged, and Naomi carried both mugs to the desk where they set their tea bags to steep.

"Yeah. He said he was waiting on an order from Weaver's."

Naomi swirled her spoon thoughtfully through her tea. "Cheryl, perhaps this is none of my business but ... did something happen between the two of you? You both seem so uncomfortable lately, but Levi refuses to speak of it."

Cheryl felt her face color furiously. She lifted her cup in an attempt to hide her embarrassment and then ended up scalding her tongue when she took too big of a sip. The coughing fit that ensued brought tears to her eyes.

Naomi rose swiftly to pat her on the back. "Oh my, are you all right?"

"I'm ... fine," Cheryl managed, swiping her tears on the napkin Naomi provided. "The tea was hotter than I expected."

When she finally managed to catch her breath, she took another, more cautious sip. "So Levi told me that he'd spoken to

Seth. Did he remember anything about the Watters brothers or what happened to them?"

Naomi watched her suspiciously over the rim of her own mug. She set the mug down and met Cheryl's gaze squarely. "He did remember them, but he could not tell us anything we did not already know. And *you* never answered my question." She wagged her finger at Cheryl. "Well?"

There was no hiding this time. Cheryl lowered her eyes, too humiliated to actually look at her friend. "To be honest... yes... something did happen."

Naomi sat back and folded her arms across her chest. "I thought so. What did he do? Did he say something to hurt your feelings? Perhaps Seth should speak to him..."

"No, no," Cheryl said quickly, "we just... reached a mutual conclusion. We both agreed that"—she averted her face—"while we may have real feelings for one another, there is no possible way anything could ever come of them."

She risked a peek at Naomi. How would she feel now that she was aware of the feelings between her and her stepson?

Her face remained placid, a slight wrinkle between her brows the only indication of the consternation brewing inside. "This was the mutual conclusion you reached?"

"That and we decided to remain friends."

"Friends."

Cheryl had never had to work so hard to control her breathing. She nodded. "That's correct."

"And you agreed to this?"

Compassion shone from Naomi's gaze, the sort of which cut directly to Cheryl's heart.

"What choice do we have?" She stopped before the pain in her heart became audible in her voice.

Naomi's heavy sigh echoed the one Cheryl felt building inside. "It is a difficult thing," she said at last. "I will not lie and say the matter will not require much prayer and consideration, but I am glad that you have been honest about your feelings." With one hand, she fingered the string on her kapp. With the other, she plucked nervously at her bottom lip. "Have you thought about what you will do if... that is... should Levi..."

Her shoulders drooped, and she eyed Cheryl sadly. "Would it break your heart to see him with someone else?"

Tears of a different sort sprang to Cheryl's eyes. She wiped them away with the same napkin and then wadded it up and stuffed it into the trash can. She drew a deep breath that did much to calm the racing of her heart and let it out slowly. "I've already thought about that, just today, in fact." She didn't add the part about meeting Ellen on their way to lunch. "Obviously, I wouldn't like it very much, but I do want what's best for Levi."

And for his family, she added silently. *For you.*

"Besides," she said after a moment, "I have other things on my plate to worry about—like tracking down Jackson Mathers again so I can ask him about his father's business dealings."

She grabbed a stack of receipts on her desk and set about putting them in proper order. It was a poor attempt at diversion, but thankfully, Naomi was too sweet to be anything less than tactful. She took her cue from Cheryl and let the subject of Levi drop.

"What exactly did you find on Jackson?" She took a sip of her tea and listened while Cheryl outlined everything from his declining subscribers to the sale of the paper and the legal battle that ensued.

"I don't know, Naomi. Something tells me Jackson Mathers may have had ulterior motives when he wrote his article about Datschel and Trampas."

"Such as?"

"I'm not sure. I mean, I know the clues are there, I just can't quite put my finger on them." She drummed her fingernails against the desk in frustration. "Anyway, I'm certain there's more to the story than what I've uncovered so far."

Naomi set aside her tea, her lips puckered as if she, too, found the situation frustrating. "This is troubling, indeed. What will you do?"

"I haven't decided, actually," she admitted. "I'd like to ask him about it, but I'm sort of hesitant about going alone. He wasn't all that pleasant the last time. Just thinking about going back to his place makes me shudder."

"You do not think he is dangerous?" she exclaimed, her eyes widening.

"Oh no, it's not that, exactly. He was just so angry and filled with bitterness. I didn't enjoy talking to him and wouldn't look forward to doing it again."

"Well, I could go with you," Naomi offered, perking up in her chair so she resembled a curious little sparrow.

Cheryl straightened. "Really?"

She gave an enthusiastic nod. "Why not? When were you thinking of going?"

"*Hmm.*" Cheryl frowned, thinking. Tomorrow was Friday—not one of the busiest days at the Swiss Miss, but to try to get someone to fill in for her tonight was certainly short notice. "Do you think Lydia would be free to help out at the store tomorrow?"

Naomi nodded. "I will ask her to be certain, but I know she is hoping to make a little extra money before Christmas. I am sure she will be happy to help."

"Great. But you will call and let me know if she has something else planned?"

"I will."

For the first time that afternoon, Cheryl could think of something besides Levi. She and Naomi finished their tea and chatted, and then Naomi left, promising to return early the next day for their visit to Jackson. Cheryl watched her go with a nervous sort of anticipation building inside her chest. As far as she was concerned, *early* couldn't come early enough.

Naomi was true to her word the next day, arriving nearly half an hour before the store opened and toting Esther and Lydia along with her in the buggy. Once the girls had stowed their heavy coats and business had settled into a slow but steady rhythm, she and Naomi headed out for New Philadelphia. As before, Cheryl was careful to have all of the information she'd gathered on Creston

Media tucked into a pocket of her purse when they walked up to Jackson's door. Through the window, she could see a TV set flickering, but it was some time before they heard shuffling steps approach and the door swung open to reveal a very rumpled Jackson Mathers. This time he looked anything but pleased to see her.

His eyes flicked from her to Naomi and back. "Miss Cooper? What are you doing here?"

"Good morning, Mr. Mathers." She turned to include Naomi. "This is my friend, Naomi Miller. May we come in for a minute?"

In response, he positioned himself between the door and the jamb, his chin jutting forward belligerently. "What for? Is this about that Watters boy? I've already told you everything that happened. I'm sorry if it doesn't please you."

Taken aback, Cheryl stammered, "Actually, Mr. Mathers, this is about something else."

He eyed her a second longer and then shook his head. "I'm afraid this isn't a good time."

"It will only take a moment," she insisted before he could close the door. "It's about your father."

Almost instantly, his frown morphed into a scowl. "My father is dead, Miss Cooper. He passed away almost twenty years ago."

"I know, and I'm sorry. I read about his passing while I was researching his holdings." She paused and then added, "His *business* holdings."

The implication was enough to make Jackson hesitate. Slowly, he opened the door but jerked his chin toward Naomi before inviting them in. "What about her? Does she know about this?"

"She does," Cheryl asserted with more calm than she felt. "She has been working with me, so I asked her to come along. I hope you don't mind."

"Fine," he grumbled, leaving the door ajar as he whirled to shuffle down the hall. "But I only have a few minutes. I'm going out."

If that were true, he certainly didn't look dressed. He wore a faded pair of gray slacks, his feet were shoved into a pair of tattered house shoes, and a robe covered a plain black T-shirt. His hair was disheveled, and he looked more like he was preparing for a nap than a trip out. Still, Cheryl held her tongue as she and Naomi followed him to the living room.

It was slightly larger than the kitchen but stuffed with dated furniture. She and Naomi huddled on a brown plaid couch while Jackson eyed them from a worn leather recliner opposite.

"Well?" he demanded at last. "What is this about?"

Cheryl eased to the edge of the couch. "Mr. Mathers, the last time I was here, you were very adamant about Datschel Watters. You said you thought there was more to his story than what he revealed to the police. Would you mind telling us why you felt that way?"

His eyes narrowed, like he was gauging her response or how much he should say. "Some might call it a reporter's instinct," he said at last, his voice growly and low.

"What would *you* call it?" Cheryl insisted.

He gave a satisfied nod, as though he deemed her answer fitting. "You're a lot like your uncle, you know that? He never would stop pushing to get what he was after either. He would have made an excellent reporter."

Cheryl wasn't fooled into thinking that a compliment. She acknowledged his comment with a tip of her head and then motioned for him to continue.

"I guess that's why I knew I had to keep digging. A man like that, so determined, had to be hiding something."

At first Cheryl was outraged by his words but quickly had to admit Uncle Ralph *was* hiding something—he was protecting Mazee and Datschel—helping them keep their relationship secret. She bit her lip and waited.

"*Hmm.*" Jackson tapped the arm of the recliner, and his eyes gleamed with interest.

"So?" Naomi asked quickly. "What did you find out?"

He turned his gaze to her. Cheryl blew out a relieved breath. With her pointed question, Naomi diverted his attention just long enough for Cheryl to collect her thoughts. When he looked back, she'd composed her features into a careful mask.

"Some things stay buried, no matter how deep you dig," he grunted.

He shrugged, a casual move that fanned Cheryl's anger. She leaned forward, pressing her balled fist into the palm of her other hand. "But the article you wrote, the cover-up that you hinted at...you mean to say you hadn't even stumbled on to some facts when you wrote the things you did?"

Her tone was more accusatory than she intended, but she couldn't help it and refused to retract the question. "Well?" she demanded. "Did you?"

His breathing had quickened, becoming a rasping wheeze that rumbled up from his chest. He wagged his finger at her but didn't speak until he'd calmed enough to form words.

"Everything I said in that article was true. Your uncle *did* try to keep me from writing about the Watters family, and he did step in when police officers arrived for questioning."

"All right then, what about Datschel?"

Cheryl's voice had begun to rise with her emotions. Next to her, Naomi cleared her throat discreetly, but Cheryl ignored her and pushed on.

"You practically accused him of murdering his brother. Do you have any idea of the impact your words had on the family? Did you ever bother to find out? What evidence did you have to say the things you did?"

Jackson leaned forward and slapped both palms on his knees. "What do I care if my stories made them uncomfortable? The truth often does that, Miss Cooper."

"It did more than make them uncomfortable," Cheryl said, her face hot. Though she was itching to pace, she kept herself firmly planted on the couch. "You destroyed a man's reputation and ripped apart a family, and for what? A sensationalized column that you couldn't prove? Where was your integrity? And why wasn't your editor checking facts?" A thought clicked in her head. "Oh, that's right, your father was your editor. You could pretty much write whatever you wanted, so long as it sold papers. Was that it?"

Jackson rose while she was still speaking and jabbed his finger toward her angrily. "I was a reporter before you were even born. I admit, I didn't have all the fancy equipment that reporters have nowadays. I couldn't Google every fact or do an Internet search every time I needed a bit of information, but I did what I could with the technology that was available at the time." He leaned toward her, his lips thinned and white. "I wrote the truth exactly as I saw it, Miss Cooper."

This time she couldn't control a sudden flash of temper. "The truth? I don't think so."

"Oh, really." He straightened and crossed his arms over his chest. "Well, you're so hooked on facts? What evidence do you have to prove that I lied?"

She shook her head. "I don't." She forged on, despite his smug smile. "I can't prove you lied or, more accurately, that you exaggerated the details of what happened that night, but I do think I know why."

His sneer grew more pronounced. He crossed his arms, ruffling the robe. "And why is that?"

Cheryl drew a slow breath. "I think you resented the fact that your father was forced to sell the paper. I think you hated the Watters family because it was Mr. Watters who bought your father out. You had a grudge against Datschel and his brother long before this story ever broke. You were looking for dirt, and you found it the night Trampas died."

The longer she spoke, the redder Jackson became. His eyes looked black with rage, and his entire body trembled. "I hated

Watters for what he did to my father," he spat then drew a long breath and pushed his shoulders back. "That doesn't mean I made up that whole story about his son and what happened with his brother. I told you, I wrote the truth as I saw it. I stand by every word I wrote."

This time Cheryl rose and crossed the floor to meet him. "If that's true, and you still believe the things you wrote were actually what happened that night, then why did you find it necessary to burn my things?"

Jackson looked genuinely taken aback. "What?" His face scrunched, and he shook his head in confusion. "What in the world are you talking about?"

"My articles, the photos, including the one you gave me...someone broke into the church and burned the entire folder."

"What church?"

"Friendship Mennonite."

"Never heard of it."

"That's not true. I told you about it the first time I came to see you. Whoever set that fire had to know I was going there to have copies made."

"And you think I did it?"

"Didn't you?"

He pointed toward the door. "I think it's about time you and your friend left."

He was throwing them out? No explanation or remorse, just anger and callous indifference as to the damage he'd caused?

Naomi placed a steadying hand on her elbow, quelling the anger that threatened to spill from her lips.

"Come, Cheryl. Mr. Mathers has given his answer."

Cheryl stared at her in mute silence.

"We must take him at his word," Naomi urged quietly, her eyes saying more than her words. They would get nothing further from Jackson Mathers, at least nothing they could trust.

Cheryl glanced at him in dismay. His lips were tightly clamped, and his hands, though gnarled and dotted with age, were bunched into fists. Naomi was right. Whether she believed him or not wasn't the point. She had no choice but to take him at his word or prove he was lying…something she could not do without evidence.

She thanked him for his time…grudgingly…and then she and Naomi left.

"Well, that was a complete waste of time," Cheryl muttered once they were in the car and headed back toward Sugarcreek.

"*Hmm*…I do not think I would call it a waste."

Cheryl lifted one eyebrow and glanced at Naomi sidelong.

"We know why he wrote the article. We can prove he was biased on the things he reported about Datschel and Trampas, which means the things he said about your onkel were also tainted. How is this waste?"

Her words repeated over and over in Cheryl's head the rest of the way home. Though she'd started out wanting only to clear Uncle Ralph's name, somehow it had also become about proving Datschel's innocence—a man she did not know and had never met—yet who had managed to win her sympathy.

Back at the store, Naomi clasped Cheryl's hands tightly. "Are you all right?"

She sighed heavily. "I guess so. It's just...nothing about this situation makes any sense."

"Not to us, and not right now. Maybe not ever. Some mysteries are not meant to be solved." She let go of Cheryl's hands and motioned toward the office. "It has been almost two weeks. Will you tell your aunt Mitzi when you speak to her?"

Cheryl slapped her palm on her forehead. "Sugar and grits. I haven't even thought about trying to reach Aunt Mitzi." Indecision warred in her brain. She wanted answers, but she didn't want to cause her aunt undue grief by bringing up painful memories.

"Pray about it," Naomi advised gently. "Seek Gotte's direction. He will show you what to do."

Remorse covered Cheryl like a blanket. Prayer was the most important thing lacking from the moment she'd started trying to discover the truth about Datschel and Trampas or Uncle Ralph. She hadn't sought God's direction. She hadn't asked for His wisdom. It was a mistake she intended to rectify.

But first...she'd ask His forgiveness.

Chapter Twenty

Cheryl felt strong and refreshed the following Sunday after spending time in prayer, followed by an uplifting worship service. Dwight Foster inquired into her progress on the history project, and though he looked concerned when she told him she'd been forced to put her research on hold, he seemed confident that she would gather the information in time for next year's festival.

Cheryl thanked him and made her way to the parking lot. For the first time in days, her mind and heart were clear of distractions and worry, and she went home knowing just what she should do.

An hour later, a fire crackled in the fireplace. There was something comforting in the sound of a fire. The hissing and popping filled the empty spaces and coaxed some of the tension from her muscles. Cheryl sat on the couch with a pen and paper in her lap and cup of tea at her elbow.

"Give me the words, Lord," she whispered before setting the pen to paper.

Dear Aunt Mitzi,

She chewed the cap on her pen. Opening her letter was the easy part. What followed would be more difficult. She drew a breath and continued writing.

There have been many times since you left for Papua New Guinea to serve as a missionary that I wished I could talk to you but never more than the past few days. I suppose it was knowing you were out of reach that made the distance seem so great this time, or maybe it was just wanting you near. Either way, I have missed you.

She flicked the end of her pen cap while she debated over telling her about the history project and then decided that part of the story could wait until they talked face-to-face.

There are many things I didn't know about you and Uncle Ralph—things from your life before I was born. I guess it never occurred to me that the two of you lived a very full lifetime before I came along. Silly, huh?

I suppose what shocks me most is that as much as the two of you loved one another, there was a period *before* you two met...when you dreamed of becoming a missionary and Uncle Ralph was consumed with life here in Sugarcreek.

This became very evident when I stumbled across an article at the library. It was about a young man named Datschel Watters and his brother Trampas. I wish I could see your face right now, to know if you remember these names or what happened to them so long ago. In case you don't... Trampas was the young Amish man who dreamed of becoming an Olympic swimmer. He drowned over forty years ago, and for a time, rumors circulated that his brother may have been responsible. The part that bothered me, however, was the insinuation that Uncle Ralph might have been involved in helping Datschel cover up his crime. I knew this couldn't be true, but I was so devastated by the implication that Naomi and I have been hard at work trying to prove his innocence. My search for answers led me to the boxes in the basement and a couple of old yearbooks.

Once again, she paused to breathe a heartfelt prayer for wisdom. At her feet, Beau watched her silently, his whiskers twitching. She reached down to give him a tickle. He responded by leaping onto her lap. When he began purring, Cheryl instantly felt a sense of calm return to her heart. The next part didn't have to be about Uncle Ralph's affection for another girl when he was in high school. She could focus on the things she'd always known—the things about him that mattered. She turned back to her letter.

I've always known what a good man Uncle Ralph was. I've always known how much he cared for others. It always made me feel good knowing he was a man who could be counted on to help when I needed him. What I had never considered was that he was the same way with everyone, that everyone in Sugarcreek looked to him as a sort of "go to" guy when it came to getting things done.

In my search for answers, I learned that Uncle Ralph came to the aid of an old high school sweetheart—a woman by the name of Mazee Stillwell. At the time, she was a Vander Huis, and she and Uncle Ralph dated for many years...until Datschel Watters came along. Mazee said she lost her heart to him not long after they met, something Uncle Ralph realized almost immediately.

Cheryl hesitated as a tiny worm of an idea began wriggling in her brain.

Mazee loved Datschel. She'd been desperate to protect him all those years ago, so much that she'd gone to an old boyfriend for help. Later she'd asked Cheryl to leave the past buried and focus on the more positive aspects of the town's history. She had access to the church and...

The pen clattered to the table. Why hadn't she thought of this before?

"Let me up, Beau," Cheryl ordered, giving the obstinate feline a shove.

He leaped to the floor and then scurried from the room, the tip of his tail flicking in irritation. Ignoring him, she carefully banked the fire and then closed the fireplace doors. With that chore done, she reached for her phone. A second later, she thought better of calling and shoved the phone into her purse while she headed for the door.

"I'm sorry, Beau," she called, hoping he'd hear her from wherever he'd gone to hide. She jammed her arms into the sleeves of her coat and grabbed her scarf. "I'll make it up to you when I get back."

She plucked her keys from a hook near the door and made a beeline for her car. Traffic was light in Sugarcreek on a Sunday afternoon, but she resisted the urge to speed. Twenty minutes later, she'd parked and was mounting the steps toward Mazee Stillwell's front door. It opened after the first ring, and she was greeted by the austere housekeeper.

"Good afternoon, Miss Cooper," Ms. Baxter said.

"Good afternoon," Cheryl said, shooting a quick peek over Ms. Baxter's shoulder into the house. "Is Mazee in?"

"She is. We're just finishing up with lunch. Is Mrs. Stillwell expecting you?"

Cheryl fingered the handle of her purse where she'd shoved her phone. "I'm afraid she's not. I didn't call first. Sorry. I hope it's not a bad time."

Ms. Baxter opened the door wider. "I will let her know you're here. Please come in."

"Thank you."

"May I take your coat?"

"Yes, thank you," Cheryl said again. She slid from her coat and gave it to Ms. Baxter along with her scarf then paced the floor while she waited for Mazee to appear. A short while later, her steady footsteps sounded in the hall.

She extended her hands, one of which wore a large bandage, and gave Cheryl a hug. "Hello, dear. What a pleasant surprise."

"I didn't come at a bad time, did I?" Cheryl said. "I didn't see you at church this morning."

"Oh...thank you for noticing." Mazee gave a slight wave of her unbandaged hand. "No, I was feeling a little under the weather and decided to stay home, but I'm much better now. Would you like to come in? I was just about to fix myself a cup of tea."

"Tea would be nice," Cheryl said.

She followed Mazee down the long hall and into an expansive kitchen. A large island surrounded by wrought-iron stools dominated the space. She pulled one of these out and sat while Mazee set the water on to boil.

When she finished, she joined Cheryl at the island. "How was the service this morning?"

"Beautiful. Pastor Lory does such a wonderful job preparing his messages week after week."

"Agreed. I was sorry to miss this morning. I was really looking forward to his series on the four Gospels." Mazee smiled. She reached for a platter of cookies at the center of the island, removed the glass dome, and offered one to Cheryl.

She shook her head and patted her waistline. "No thanks. I'm in my large jeans as it is."

Mazee chuckled and replaced the lid then pushed the cookies away with her good hand. "Well, that's one good thing about getting old, I suppose. I don't worry quite so much about my waistline as I did in my younger days."

"What happened to your hand, by the way?" Cheryl asked. "Did you hurt yourself?"

"This?" She wriggled her bandaged fingers. "Oh, this is nothing."

"Did you cut yourself?"

Mazee slid off the stool and went to check on the water. "Uh...no. It's just a little burn. I scalded myself making coffee the other day."

Cheryl perked up on her stool. "Really? I didn't notice it when we stopped by earlier this week."

Mazee held up two tea bags. "Orange spice or Earl Grey?"

"Earl Grey, please."

Mazee ripped the top part off the package and dropped the tea bag into the cup she carried to Cheryl. "Here you go, dear. Would you like some cream or sugar?"

"Just a little sugar, please," Cheryl said, mindful that while Mazee's demeanor remained pleasant, she had managed to avoid discussing the specifics of how and when she'd burned her hand.

When she'd returned with the sugar bowl, Mazee resumed her seat and took a sip of her tea. "Mmm. I love a good cup of tea in the afternoon. So much better for me than coffee. I've noticed it makes me much more jittery as I've gotten older. Never used to affect me before."

"My mother says the same thing," Cheryl said, spooning a bit of sugar into her cup.

They exchanged pleasantries for several minutes, but noting the way Mazee fidgeted with the string on her tea bag and the way she refused to hold her gaze long, Cheryl sensed both of them were aware that the real subject of discussion had yet to be broached.

"So tell me what brings you by today." Mazee set her tea down, the sound a gentle click against the marble island top.

Finally. Cheryl set her cup down alongside Mazee's and took in a deep breath. "Actually, Mazee, it's about Datschel Watters."

She waited, half expecting her to protest and surprised when she didn't. Instead, Mazee hung her head and turned on her stool to rest her elbows on the marble.

"I thought as much," she said quietly. "To be honest, I'm a bit surprised you haven't stopped by before now."

"Really?" Her heart thumped inside her chest.

One of Mazee's shoulders lifted in a shrug. "You're a smart girl, Cheryl. It really was only a matter of time before you came to talk to me again."

Cheryl leaned toward her and lightly tapped the bandages on her hand. "Mazee, what happened to your hand?"

The kitchen fell silent, the only sounds the hum of the refrigerator and the ticking of the hands on the clock above the stove.

"I *did* burn it," she said at last, almost with a note of childlike apology in her voice.

"But you didn't do it making coffee."

She shook her head. "No, I didn't."

Cheryl thought back to the day she and Naomi had come to tell Mazee her photographs had been destroyed. Though she hadn't worn a bandage then, she'd very obviously favored her uninjured hand. Cheryl simply hadn't noticed it then as she did now and didn't ask because she'd been so wrapped up searching for details about Uncle Ralph.

She leaned forward. "Was it at the church? The day that Naomi and I stopped by, were you just getting back from there?"

Remorse washed across her face. She held up her hand, palm out. "Before I tell you why I burned those things, will you give me a chance to explain what led me to do it?"

Cheryl nodded slowly. While she'd suspected that it had been Mazee when she drove over here, it was still surprising to hear her declare it so plainly.

Suddenly, Mazee looked very small perched on her stool, her face wrinkled and careworn. She blew out a sigh that seemed to draw every last bit of breath from her lungs, and when she finished, she shook her head slowly.

"I tried for months to find Datschel after he disappeared from Sugarcreek. I left my home, my friends, my family, and scoured every place I could think of that he might have gone. I even went to his father." Her lips turned in a wry grin. "Though I can't say he was happy to see me, I think he was glad that I was at least trying to find him. Of course, he never actually said so."

This at least seemed in keeping with what Cheryl knew of Datschel Watters's father. Even Jackson had painted him as hard and unmoving. She fidgeted uncomfortably. "What about Datschel's sister?"

"Violet?"

Cheryl nodded.

Mazee frowned. "I never understood how she could let her father drive Datschel away the way he did. To stand by and do nothing…" She pressed her lips together tightly, stopping the bitter words before they could leave her mouth.

"If it makes you feel any better," Cheryl said softly, "Violet has lived with that regret ever since Datschel disappeared. She told me so when I went to see her about the fire. She misses her brother, Mazee. I know she would do anything to see him again and know that he is okay."

Gradually, the tense lines eased from Mazee's features and she offered a shaky smile. "That does make me feel a little better I suppose. It's more than just knowing that someone else missed him as much as I did. I wanted to know that his family loved him."

Cheryl reached out and placed her hand over Mazee's arm. "What happened to Datschel after he left Sugarcreek? Surely you know?"

Tears welled in her eyes. "Actually, I don't. I never found out where he went, or what he did."

"Mazee..."

"It's true." She gave a stubborn shake of her head. "I lived for years thinking he'd died, or been arrested, or worse. I honestly had no idea what had become of him until..."

Cheryl's heart rate sped. She stilled and urged her to continue. "Until?"

Mazee's chin rose a fraction. She covered Cheryl's hand with her uninjured one. "First, I want you to know that I loved my husband, Cheryl."

When she nodded, Mazee pressed on.

"But if I am honest, I would have to say there was always a part of me that wondered what would have happened between Datschel and me if..." She brushed the idea away with a swipe of her hand. "I have always carried a bit of my love for Datschel in my heart. He remained a part of me even after my children were born, like a figure in a dream I remembered from long ago." She paused, her gaze distant. "And then Muddy appeared."

Cheryl gasped. Inside, her chest felt like Mazee had slammed her with a bat. "I don't understand. What does Muddy...?"

She broke off, her eyes widening as realization dawned. "Muddy *Watters?*"

Mazee nodded slowly. "I recognized him the moment he walked into Sugarcreek. Behind the long hair and beard and the sad, haunted eyes, I could still see the sweet, gentle man I once loved. I suppose that's why I've been so angry with Violet. I couldn't understand why she didn't see as well."

A picture of Muddy flashed into Cheryl's mind, exactly as Mazee described. At last, she knew what it was about the photo of Datschel that had seemed so familiar. "But...where had he been all that time? Why did he suddenly decide to come back to Sugarcreek, and why didn't he tell anyone?"

She pressed both hands to the cool marble and shrugged. "I told you the truth when I said I didn't know where Datschel disappeared to. The years between his absence and now will more than likely forever be a mystery."

Cheryl blinked, processing what she'd heard and trying hard to organize her thoughts into some kind of order. "But Mazee, aren't you curious to know where he's been?"

"Of course."

"Have you talked to him? Why did he wait so long to come back? Does anyone else know who he is? And what about his sister? Aren't you going to tell her who he is?" Her questions came faster now, gushing like floodwaters over a levy.

Mazee held up her hand, halting the flow. "Muddy doesn't know that I know who he is. Though I've seen him talk to others, he and I have never spoken. We never will, unless he decides to break his self-imposed silence toward me. And if he decides to reveal who he is, that will be his choice."

"W-what?" Confusion roiled in her head. "But if you still love him...why wouldn't you tell him?"

Mazee lowered her gaze. She fingered the gold rim of her cup, her lips curving in a sad smile that tugged at Cheryl's heart. "Datschel left me once. As much as I loved him, it wasn't enough to make him stay. Who is to say he wouldn't leave again?"

"But...but..." Cheryl sat up straight and waved her hands helplessly.

She nodded. "I know this is hard to understand. Twenty years ago, I wouldn't have believed it myself." She leaned forward, her eyes wide and earnest. "I was angry when Muddy first came back to town, Cheryl. I couldn't understand why he didn't come to me, why he didn't explain where he'd gone. At first, I thought it was because of Jonathan, my husband. But then he died and still, Muddy kept his distance." She grinned wryly. "I suppose I wouldn't be human if I said that didn't hurt. I almost confronted him then."

"Why didn't you?"

"I knew there had to be a reason," she replied, her gaze thoughtful. "I spent countless hours trying to figure it out, and then one day it just didn't matter anymore. I realized I *could* live never having the answers to how or why. I was just grateful to have him at all."

Have him? Cheryl frowned. How did seeing him around town and bumping into him at church count as "having him"?

"I see I've confused you." Surprisingly, Mazee chuckled. The sound caught Cheryl off guard, and she stilled long enough to really think.

"The money envelopes that Muddy collects from the church...those are from you?"

She nodded.

"How long?"

A corner of her mouth rose in a crooked smile. "I suppose it started the day I first realized I wasn't angry anymore. I'd let go of my hurt. With that out of the way, I was finally able to see him for who he is, and not who I wanted him to be."

Cheryl thought back to the ride she'd given Muddy and the homeless shelter where he'd gone to deliver canned goods. She leaned toward Mazee, studying her carefully as she struggled to understand this curious woman she thought she knew. "Do you even know what he does with the money?"

"I have no idea," Mazee confessed matter-of-factly. "I've never asked, and I never will. It's enough to know I'm helping him."

Cheryl couldn't help it—she had to ask the questions simmering on her tongue. "Why, Mazee? Why is it so important to you to try to take care of someone who doesn't even realize that you know who they are?"

She pondered this a moment, her brows drawn into a line as she mulled her response. "I...suppose...it was my way of making up for failing to do what I wanted to do all those years ago."

"Which was?"

"Protect him," she answered. She spread her hands, her voice lowered plaintively. "It makes no sense, I know, but leaving money for him at the church was the only way I could still feel close to him. Still feel as though I shared something with him of our past.

Something that wasn't ugly and tainted by hurt and shame. I knew he would never accept it if he knew it came from me, but through the church…"

She trailed off, and Cheryl let the silence linger between them a moment. At last she laid her hand over Mazee's fingers, stilling their restless thrumming against the marble countertop.

"Mazee, were you still protecting him when you went to the church and burned my files?"

She swallowed, and her eyes, which she'd managed to keep dry throughout, now filled with tears. "I'm so sorry, Cheryl. It was a terrible thing to do, but after all these years, I couldn't bear the thought of someone accidently digging up the past and driving Muddy away again. If that happens, I know I will never see him again. He'll disappear and never come back. I went to the church to see what you'd been working on, but when I looked through your file and saw all of the articles on Muddy…"

"It was Uncle Ralph," Cheryl corrected quickly. "I wasn't trying to dig up information on Muddy. I only wanted to clear Uncle Ralph's name, although I will admit, a part of me felt sorry for Muddy and wanted to prove his innocence."

Her brows rose. "So you don't believe he was responsible for his brother's death?"

The hope in her voice was tangible. Cheryl shook her head. "There was something about his face, the hurt I read in his eyes—I just couldn't believe he'd done what Jackson Mathers implied. Deep down, I just knew what happened was an accident and wanted to find a way to prove it if I could."

"Of course," Mazee said quietly. "I should have realized you would never treat a person's life so carelessly." She sighed. "I was simply too afraid to lose what little part I play in Muddy's life to risk telling you the truth. I'm sorry, Cheryl."

"I am too." Cheryl clasped Mazee's hand and gave it a tight squeeze. "What will you do now?"

Mazee squeezed back, and for the first time in many days, she seemed to have the weight lifted from her shoulders. She smiled. "Things will go on as before, I suppose. I will continue to help Muddy when I can and hope that…someday…he'll finally be free enough of the guilt from his past to come to me."

"And if that never happens?" Cheryl asked, partly out of concern for Mazee and partly out of fear that she'd be faced with a similar choice.

A tiny bit of sorrow returned to her eyes. "It is not easy, loving someone from afar. There have been times when I felt certain I couldn't do it. Other times, I clung to my hope like a lifeline. In the end, it was Datschel I cared about. It was his welfare that kept me silent. Do you understand?"

Cheryl gave a slow nod. She did understand. Somewhat.

She slid off her stool and waited while Mazee did the same. When she opened her arms, Cheryl slid into them, glad that though there had been secrets and misunderstandings, she hadn't lost a friend.

"I'm sorry, Mazee," she whispered. "For everything."

By "everything," she meant more than just the events of recent weeks. She was sorry for the accident that had driven a wedge between Mazee and the man she now knew as Muddy. She was sorry for the anger and guilt that had driven him out of Sugarcreek, and for the ache of the powerful love that brought him back. Most of all, she was sorry for the things that still kept them apart, even as it bound them together.

Mazee seemed to understand this. She thanked Cheryl quietly and then peered into her eyes for a long moment before she spoke.

"It isn't easy, giving up the man you love. But sometimes... sometimes letting them go is how you can love them the most. I just felt like you needed to hear that."

Cheryl's thoughts winged to Levi, and her heart grew heavy inside her chest. Though it pained her to realize it, she knew exactly what Mazee meant.

CHAPTER TWENTY-ONE

Beau greeted Cheryl with a loud meow when she arrived home. He jumped from the back of the couch where he'd been watching from the window and scurried across the carpet to rub against her legs as she pushed open the door, his happy purr a welcome rumble.

"Hey, buddy," she said, scooping him up and pressing his soft fur against her cheek. "I'm sorry I haven't been paying much attention to you lately. I've been a little preoccupied."

She stepped over two days' worth of newspapers, realizing as she did that she needed to make a trip to the mailbox.

"But first, I think we'll get you a little treat, eh, Beau?" she said, burrowing her fingers into the tuft of fur on his chest. He responded by running his rough tongue over her knuckles.

"You agree, huh?"

Cheryl chuckled as she carried him into the kitchen. It was true, she hadn't been paying as much attention to Beau as she'd like, but fortunately for her, cats were often more forgiving than people. Retrieving a tin from the top of the refrigerator, she pulled out a tuna-flavored treat and set it on the counter for Beau to devour at his leisure.

"I'll be right back," she said, running her hand over his back and down his tail. "I'm just going out to the mailbox."

He eyed her, unblinking, then decided he was more interested in the treat. His whiskers twitched as he carried it from the counter to the floor and then out of the kitchen.

"So much for missing me," Cheryl said with a wry grin.

She ambled to the mailbox. Though it was Sunday, it was indeed quite full after not being cleared two days in a row. She sorted through the first few letters as she walked slowly back into the house, but it was a familiar postmark and a bright yellow envelope that made her hurry the last few steps.

"A letter from Aunt Mitzi." Cheryl held the prized item aloft. "She must have known I'd be missing her."

She crossed to the table where her own unfinished letter waited. Shoving it aside, she ripped open the envelope and began reading.

My darling Cheryl,

Instantly, a bit of the uncertainty and tension tumbled from Cheryl's shoulders. Hearing Aunt Mitzi's voice always made things right, even if it was only through a letter.

What a month it has been! The work here seems never-ending at times, yet I have never felt so confident that I am in God's will and doing His work. Last week we helped a visiting doctor administer immunizations to children who have never seen a needle. It was quite a job calming their parents' fears and assuring them that what we were giving them was medicine. I even had one protective father demand that the shot be administered to him first so he could be certain it would not harm his son. When it was all over, both of them were wearing matching Band-Aids and proud smiles.

Cheryl smiled as she read those words. What a joy it must have been to see such selfless love demonstrated. She read on.

For some strange reason, this papa reminded me so much of my Ralph. They looked nothing alike, and yet I sensed some of the same characteristics in him that I loved in Ralph over the years. I suppose it was the same caring nature, the strong protective instincts, that have made my thoughts linger on times past as they have not in many months. I feel I have been beyond blessed to have known such depth of love from a man like Ralph Porter.

Here, the ink was smudged a bit, as though a tear had been wiped from the page. Cheryl felt her own eyes burn, but she blinked back the tears that threatened and continued reading.

I won't lie and say we didn't have our struggles. Though we longed for them, Ralph and I never had children. We disagreed about becoming missionaries. And the list goes on. Yet time has eased the memory of those trials and left instead a warm place in my heart for the years we spent learning to love and trust one another to a degree I never imagined possible. I can say without hesitation that I do not regret one day of my life with Ralph, nor would I trade one experience. I am glad for the life I have lived, and that, I suppose, is the trademark of a soul given fully to the Lord.

This indeed has become my prayer for the people here, and for you as well, my darling niece. I pray that you know the joy, the peace, and the confidence that comes with having lived your life walking closely with God. Ralph knew this. I have come to know it. I earnestly hope you will as well.

> With all of my love and affection,
> Your Aunt Mitzi

For several minutes, Cheryl sat rereading Mitzi's letter and adding her own tearstains to the wrinkled pages. The message was not uncommon. Aunt Mitzi's letters were often filled with words of hope and encouragement. What surprised Cheryl was her almost uncanny knack for speaking directly to every situation Cheryl found herself in, whether she knew what was happening in Sugarcreek or not.

Drawing a shuddering breath, she laid Mitzi's letter aside and picked up her own. Grasping one edge, she tore it in two then bunched it into a ball and tossed it into the trash.

Aunt Mitzi was right.

Cheryl needed to learn to walk in joy and peace. She couldn't do that by hiding from her emotions. Confidence would only come from tackling her problems head-on. Right now, that meant dealing with her feelings for Levi. Openly. Honestly.

Her mind made up, Cheryl rose from the table and went in search of her coat and keys.

For the second time in weeks, she knew exactly what she had to do . . . and whom she needed to see. It wouldn't be easy, but there was one place she'd find true peace.

She needed to go to the Millers' farm.

CHAPTER TWENTY-TWO

Cheryl had never been so nervous heading to the Millers' farm as she was on this day. She drove past the corn maze, her chest rising and falling as she worked to steady her breathing. Today the babbling creek held no charm, the old covered bridge did not remind her of romantic walks, and when she reached the farmhouse with its wraparound porch, she counted to five before exiting her car.

It was early evening, but not too early. And it was a Sunday, which meant Seth and Levi and the others could be finished with their chores and the family gathered around a fire. Would she be interrupting? Would they welcome her presence, or would they wonder why she'd felt compelled to come out unannounced on a day they typically set aside for family?

Crisp air bit her lungs as she crossed the yard and climbed the steps leading to the porch. The snow and ice had been cleared here, but icicles dripped from the eaves, a reminder that some things were inevitable... like winter... and this meeting.

Cheryl pulled her gloves from her fingers and knocked—a habit she'd almost forgotten but felt obliged to renew today. She waited, heart pounding, until footsteps sounded opposite and the door swung open.

Naomi wiped her hands on the apron covering her plain blue dress. "Cheryl?"

She glanced past her, over her shoulder, as though she expected to see someone else, for what other explanation could there be for her standing on the porch waiting to be invited in?

Her confused smile grew. "What are you doing...?"

"Naomi, have you got a minute? I know it's getting near to suppertime, but I'd really like to talk to you, if that's okay."

Cheryl's words stumbled over themselves, and she felt her face grow hot, but she lowered her voice and forged on. "It's about Levi, so if this isn't a good time..."

She'd...what? Come back later? Wait until tomorrow? Suddenly, she felt very foolish.

She clutched her purse tightly to her side. "You know, maybe I should just..."

"It is a fine time," Naomi interrupted, her eyes gentle and understanding. "Would you like me to fetch Levi?"

"No," she said, almost too loudly. She shot a glance inside, glad when the hall remained empty. "No, thank you. I, uh, I came to see you."

"I see," Naomi said, though her confused frown indicated she didn't really and only said so to be kind. She grasped Cheryl by the hand and drew her inside. To her relief, no male voices drifted from the kitchen or living room, only Elizabeth's and Esther's and they seemed to be involved in a very animated discussion about sewing patterns.

"I have a pot of *kaffee* brewing." Naomi took Cheryl's coat and gloves and hung them by the door. "You look like you could use a cup."

A gentle smile accompanied the words, easing a bit of the anxiety from Cheryl's chest. She followed Naomi to the large kitchen table where she'd shared family meals and had many discussions in recent weeks.

Naomi poured them both a cup of coffee then settled into a chair next to Cheryl's. "Now, what is troubling you, my friend?"

Cheryl took a hesitant sip of her coffee, hoping the stout brew would lend her a bit of courage. Instead she ended up scalding her tongue. Sputtering a bit, she set down her cup.

"Ach, I should have warned you," Naomi said, hurrying to the cupboard for a napkin and a glass she half filled with water. She carried both back to the table. "Are you all right?"

"I'm fine." Cheryl thanked her for the water, took a sip, and then motioned toward the living room. "Where are the men?"

Naomi's smile reached all the way up to lend a twinkle to her eyes. "Seth is in the barn with Levi and the boys. They are working on a project for me, but they will not tell me what it is and I am not allowed to venture down there until it is finished." Her smile faded as her gaze searched the angles of Cheryl's face. "Are you all right? Is this about your uncle Ralph?"

"Not really," she said, feeling more miserable and confused by the minute. She sighed heavily and pushed her cup away. "Although I did speak to Mazee Stillwell earlier today. You're never going to believe this, but it was her who burned my things."

Naomi's eyes grew round, and Cheryl nodded.

"I know. I was shocked too, although when I think about it, she was the obvious answer."

"But why did she do it? Why did she not just ask for her things back if she wanted them?"

"She didn't want them," Cheryl explained. "She was concerned about protecting Muddy."

"Who?"

"The homeless man..."

Sensing she needed to explain further, Cheryl backtracked and shared everything she'd learned from Mazee, including Muddy's real identity.

"Muddy is Datschel Watters." Naomi shook her head in disbelief. "All this time, he has been right here in our midst." Her eyebrows rose. "Did Mazee say where he was before he came back to Sugarcreek?"

"She says she doesn't know, and I believe her." Cheryl's heart began to thump as she reached the point where she needed to explain the reason behind her visit. "Anyway, I really do think that everything Mazee did was out of concern for the man she once loved... and still does. She made a choice, Naomi. When Datschel came back to town, Mazee made a conscious choice to respect his wishes. She didn't reveal his identity. Everything she's done since then is in support of that decision."

Naomi pondered this quietly for a moment. "It takes a very strong woman to keep to such a commitment out of love for a man she might never have a life with."

"I agree." Cheryl stared at her friend. "You and Seth are like that—loving each other selflessly, putting each other first, caring for one another unconditionally. I see it every day in the way you treat each other."

A blush colored Naomi's cheeks. She pressed her fingers to her face and lowered her gaze. "My husband has taught me what it means to love without reservation as Gott does. I am grateful to Him for giving me such a man."

Cheryl's throat felt tight. She swallowed a sudden knot and pushed on. "Aunt Mitzi and Uncle Ralph shared the same kind of love and commitment, and so do my mom and dad." She fidgeted on her chair. "I guess what I'm trying to say is, I've had a pretty great cloud of witnesses when it comes to loving someone deeply and with all of your heart."

Puzzlement shone in the bunching of her eyebrows. "This is a goot thing, ja?"

"It is," Cheryl agreed. "I just haven't been so sure I was ready to do the same...until now."

Naomi peered at her silently, her gaze steady and assessing.

"I spoke with Levi," Cheryl admitted quietly. "A couple of days ago, when you asked me if something had happened between us? We told each other how we feel, but we also came to a decision."

"And what did you decide?" Naomi asked, a tad breathlessly. Her chair creaked as she leaned in, her face tight with anticipation.

Heat flooded Cheryl's face. Her hands shook, and her mouth felt dry. Still, the time had come to be honest with her friend, and that meant telling her everything.

"I care about Levi, Naomi, but I'm not sure it's the same way you and Seth care about each other, or the way Mazee cares about

Datschel...at least not yet. And maybe not ever." She sucked in a breath and twined her fingers tightly in her lap. "You see, Levi and I both realize that being together would mean that one of us had to change and...well...I'm just not sure that a change like that should take place simply because two people want to be together."

"I see." Naomi blew out a slow breath. "I am very sorry, Cheryl."

She shook her head. "There's more. Naomi, for the past several weeks, I've been questioning God's plan for me. I've been praying about my feelings for Levi, praying that God would change my heart and make me want the things He wants for me, praying that I remain in His perfect will. But today..."

She paused to let the burning in her throat pass. Finally, she looked up and met Naomi's gaze.

"Today I realized I've been going about it all wrong."

She drew back, uncertainty warring with concern on her face. "What do you mean?"

"I've been too focused on how I feel and the things I'm doing." Her voice shook, but her determination only grew stronger. She lifted her chin. "From now on, I'm going to start praying for Levi. I'm going to pray that God leads him in the path He wants for him, and I'm going to ask that God reveal to *him* what He wants for the two of us. That's how Aunt Mitzi loved Ralph, and I think that's what you would do for Seth, right? You want the best for him, and that includes seeking God's best for him."

Naomi nodded, her lips and chin twitching with emotion.

"And Mazee...she's another example of someone doing everything she can for the man she loves. That includes giving him the space he needs for as long as he needs it, even if it means they'll never be together."

Cheryl unclasped her hands and laid them on the table, realizing as she did so that she was finally able to let go of the hold she'd had on her plans and hopes and dreams and give them over fully to God.

She gave a curt, adamant nod. "Well, I think it's past time I followed the example of the witnesses God has surrounded me with. I think it's time I started demonstrating selfless love for God and...for Levi. As for the rest? Well, that's no longer up to me." She shrugged helplessly and gave a self-deprecating laugh. "I've sort of made a mess of things so far anyway."

Cheryl held her breath while she waited for Naomi to respond. Would she be surprised by her confession? Would she be angry?

Relief flooded her when Naomi reached out to cover Cheryl's hands, her fingers strong yet gentle, her gaze soothing and kind.

"Danki, Cheryl. I appreciate your honesty and forthrightness in including me in your plans and feelings for my stepson. I admit, I have been a little fearful, wondering if...how..."

She smiled sadly. "My Seth lost one child to an Englischer. Though the two of them have worked things out now, it was hard for a time. My heart broke seeing how he grieved for Sarah. I would not wish to see him go through such heartache again, even though we all have grown to love and care for you. You understand?"

She did, but hearing the words from Naomi's lips still hurt. She blinked rapidly and lowered her head.

"Ne, Cheryl." Naomi placed her fingers beneath her chin and lifted. "Do not be sad. Gotte has a plan for you and Levi, for sure and for certain. I cannot say I am confident on how He will work all of this out, but I do believe He wants the best for both of you, as His Holy Book says."

She paused, her mouth working as she framed her next words. "I think I could not ask for a better daughter than you, but if that is not Gotte's plan, then I believe it is because He wants you to have the kind of love you seek. One that is selfless and unconditional. If you will wait and trust in His plan, if you will delight yourself in the Lord, He shall give thee the desires of thine heart. There is no greater promise than this, ain't so?"

The tears that had been accumulating since their conversation began suddenly spilled over on to Cheryl's cheeks. She mopped them up with a napkin then allowed Naomi to wrap her in a warm, satisfying hug.

"How did you do it, Naomi?" Cheryl asked when they parted. "How did you find the strength to wait for Seth to be ready to love again? And how did you even know things would work out?"

Naomi's sigh was sincere and heartfelt. "Ach, I wish I could say I was patient. The truth is, I spent many nights wetting my pillow with my tears and wearying Gott with my many prayers. In the end, He heard my cries. I know He will hear yours as well."

She squeezed Cheryl's shoulder, her next words more profound than any Cheryl had heard her speak before.

"Be honest before your Gotte, Cheryl, and do not hold anything back, even the tiniest thing you hide in your heart. Tell Him your fears, your anxieties, your hopes. Trust them all to Him, and He will guide your steps. He is just waiting for you to ask."

Cheryl nodded, glad she'd made the decision to speak to Naomi, and even gladder still to have her peace and confidence restored. She would seek God as Naomi had, again and again, until she was certain of His answer.

Footsteps sounded outside the window, accompanied by several male voices, all loud with excitement and teasing. A second later, the kitchen door swung open. Cheryl rose with a greeting on her lips, expecting Seth.

Instead, she stood face-to-face with Levi.

CHAPTER TWENTY-THREE

Cheryl's arms hung limply at her sides as she stood blinking up at Levi. In a single deft move, he swept the broad-brimmed hat from his head with one hand and ran his fingers through his ruffled hair with the other.

She shifted back a step. "Hi." The word sounded puny in her ears, but at the moment, it was all she could manage.

"Hi."

That he repeated the inadequate greeting was not lost on her.

"Come." Naomi waved to Caleb, Esther, and the others. "Wash up and join me in the living room. We will give Cheryl and Levi space to talk."

His eyebrows rose, and Cheryl felt a fleeting embarrassment wash over her. "I . . . um . . . had a little chat with your stepmother."

Oh, for a hole to open up in the floor! Most likely he thought she'd been whining to Naomi. Or maybe he thought she'd come bearing tales. Or maybe . . .

"I am glad."

He waited while the others cleared the room and then signaled toward the table. "Would you like to sit down?"

Not trusting the weakness in her knees, she nodded and joined him at the table, where he pulled out a chair to seat her and then claimed another chair for himself.

"I am glad that you spoke to Maam. She is a wise, godly woman, and you can trust her advice."

"That's it?" Cheryl hardly trusted herself to speak. "I figured you'd be irritated with me."

"Ne. I am not."

He said it so quickly, the ensuing silence seemed almost sharp.

He lowered his gaze, and his voice, when he spoke, was filled with a hollow sort of sadness that pricked Cheryl's heart.

"You have been on my mind a lot recently."

"I...h-have?"

He nodded. "I am glad that we have a chance to talk now."

"Me too." She rubbed her palms against her pant legs, wondering if he was as nervous as she. "I know the last time we talked, we said..."

He shook his head, cutting her off before she could finish. "I have thought about what we said."

He laid his hat on the table and then leaned forward, his hands clasped and his elbows resting against his knees. "I am not happy just letting things between us go unspoken. It is not fitting to try to hide from the way things are, and...I do not think it is fair...to either of us."

"Okay."

Okay? Cheryl swallowed past a hefty lump in her throat. She wasn't exactly waxing eloquent, but at the moment, she was just glad she'd managed to speak at all.

He shook his head. "So I have made a decision. From today on, I have decided to begin praying for you, Cheryl. For both of us, and not just myself. I am going to seek Gotte's will for you because I want you to find peace and happiness, even if..."

He stumbled to a halt, but Cheryl had heard enough. Her lips twitched with the beginnings of a smile. "Really?"

He blinked, his confusion at her response evident. "Ja. But..."

It was her turn to shake her head. "No, Levi, you don't understand. I came to the same conclusion today. That's what I was talking to Naomi about."

He leaned back in his chair, his frown clearing. "Oh."

She couldn't resist a slight giggle. "That's all you have to say?"

"I guess...I suppose I thought my idea was so goot it would take you aback."

They both laughed then, freely, like they hadn't done in a long time. It was a good sound, and pleasant, and it filled Cheryl with renewed hope.

When she caught her breath, she said, "You know, I'm really glad to know that God is working in both of us, at the same time, I mean. Not that He wouldn't be working in you, it's just He's teaching us the same lesson, at the same time..." She broke off and sighed in frustration. "You know what I mean."

"I do." He twisted in his chair to rest his clasped hands on the table. "It is like the parables. Jesus may have spoken them to one person, but another listening might have learned just as much."

"Yeah. Kind of like that."

They shared a smile—something Cheryl had been missing lately.

She fidgeted with the hem of her shirt nervously. "Levi, can I ask you a question?"

He turned his gaze to her. "Of course."

She struggled with the words and finally managed to force them out. "What about Ellen?"

"Ellen?" He lowered his eyebrows in a frown.

She swallowed and forged on. "That day we met her in town and you wanted to speak to her father, remember?"

Understanding dawned in his eyes. "Ach...I see. He owns the land across from the petting zoo."

"The land you're thinking of buying," she said, hopefully.

He nodded.

"So that's what you wanted to talk to him about?"

"What else?"

Suddenly, her cheeks felt very warm. Levi apparently noticed and dropped his gaze. Reaching for his hat, he worked the brim between his fingers, round and round.

"Ellen is much too young, Cheryl, and even if she were not, she is not the girl for me."

Never had any words made her feel as relieved as his did in that moment. Even with things as yet unsettled between them, she couldn't bear the thought of him with someone else. But where did that leave them and the choices they had already made?

"Levi," she hesitated, giving herself time to work up the courage to continue, "are you happy with the decision we made not to act on our feelings?"

Her breathing had grown shallow, so her words sounded rushed, but if he noticed, he did not comment.

His gaze fell to his hands, and he began picking at the edge of his fingernail, a move that would quickly lead to a hangnail if he didn't stop.

"I believe Gott has a plan for me, Cheryl, just as He has a plan for you. What that plan is, I do not yet know, but I am willing to wait for it." He lifted his eyes to meet hers. "And you?"

"I'm glad you feel that way, Levi," she said quietly. "I couldn't agree more."

"And if He shows us another way? Would you..." He hesitated and licked his lips nervously. "That is...I would like to think..."

She smiled and shook her head. "Let's not venture there. For now, let's just do what we set out to do and keep our feelings from ruining our friendship, okay?"

His gaze searched hers, his blue eyes intense and earnest. "Okay," he said at last, and then more confidently, "Okay."

He stood, and Cheryl rose with him. Hugging was not allowed, but shaking hands seemed awkward and unnatural. Instead they exchanged a smile, one that spoke of shared heartache and longing but also a quiet sort of truce, at least for the time being.

"I'll see you later, Levi. Will you tell Naomi good-bye for me?"

"I will. Good night, Cheryl."

"Good night."

Rather than going toward the front of the house through the living room, Cheryl exited through the kitchen. As she walked through the yard, she heard Levi's voice join with the rest of his family, a joyous melody she knew wouldn't be complete without his strong tenor in the mix.

So this was what it meant to love someone from afar... to always be near but never close, always caring but never truly free to let it show.

She glanced up at the stars shining overhead. They seemed brighter here on the Millers' farm, away from the streetlights and headlights. Cheryl felt she could almost reach out and touch them. She couldn't, of course. To do so would be impossible. But she could admire them. She could bask in their glow. And she could be thankful for the times when they shone just for her. Like tonight. Or every night, if she just stopped long enough to look.

"Okay, Lord," she whispered.

She didn't need to say more. After all, the God of the universe surely understood what she meant.

For now, she would simply wait on God. It was, after all, the best thing she could do. She would try her hardest to walk in obedience until He showed her the path He wanted her to take, even if it led her to a small town like Sugarcreek or halfway around the world to Papua New Guinea. She would listen, and wait, and trust.

And she would love from afar.

AUTHOR LETTER

Dear Reader,

Recently, my husband offered me the chance of a lifetime...the chance to choose where *I* wanted to go on vacation. Anywhere. Just the two of us. A second honeymoon of sorts. With a broad spectrum of places to choose from spread out before me, I found I didn't even hesitate. I knew where I wanted to go.

I have to laugh, thinking back on the expression on his face when I told him I wanted to go to Sugarcreek, Ohio, but I was determined to see it and experience for myself the sights and sounds and people I'd only written about. And so, with surprisingly little argument from my husband, we packed our suitcases and headed north to the Carlisle Inn, a gracious little gem perched on the outskirts of Sugarcreek. If you've never been, I highly recommend you visit. It was by far the most beautiful, restful place we've ever stayed, and the staff were both friendly and accommodating.

Once in Sugarcreek, my husband and I picked up a handful of maps and set off to discover what there was to do in Amish country on a Sunday afternoon. Don't laugh...we actually found the drive through the acres and acres of carefully maintained farmland to be quite enjoyable and relaxing! More importantly, I got to see with my own eyes the things Cheryl Cooper saw when she first came to Sugarcreek.

Afterward, my husband and I popped into Park Street Pizza for a delectable bite of their famous Rueben Pizza—the same pizza Cheryl nibbled on with her date, Levi Miller, in *Home Sweet Sugarcreek*. I have to admit, I probably looked pretty silly gawking about the place, imagining where my characters sat, what they said, whom they saw. I was also honored to do a book signing at the Honey Bee Café, another one of Cheryl's favorite places to eat. It was all quite surreal and very much a dream come true for this author gal.

Of course, I couldn't leave Ohio without snapping a picture against the giant billboard that first welcomed me—and Cheryl— to Sugarcreek. It will forever serve as a reminder of that magical

moment when the places I'd written about sprang to life and when I could, however briefly, step into the pages of my very own books. I hope you'll join me there!

May God bless you,
Elizabeth Ludwig

About the Author

Elizabeth Ludwig is an award-winning author whose work has been featured on *Novel Rocket, More to Life Magazine*, and *Christian Fiction Online Magazine*. Her first novel, *Where the Truth Lies* (coauthored with Janelle Mowery), earned her the 2008 IWA Writer of the Year Award. This book was followed in 2009 by "I'll Be Home for Christmas," part of the Christmas anthology collection *Christmas Homecoming*.

In 2011, her second mystery, *Died in the Wool* (coauthored with Janelle Mowery), was nominated for a Carol Award. In 2012, the Edge of Freedom series released from Bethany House Publishers. Books one and two, *No Safe Harbor* and *Dark Road Home*, respectively, earned four stars from the RT Book Reviews. Book three in the series, *Tide and Tempest*, received top honors with four-and-one-half stars and was recently named a finalist for the Gayle Wilson Award of Excellence. Elizabeth was also named a finalist in the 2015 Selah Awards for her novella "One Holy Night," part of the best-selling anthology collection *Christmas Comes to Bethlehem, Maine*.

Elizabeth is an accomplished speaker and teacher, often attending conferences and seminars where she lectures on editing for fiction writers, crafting effective novel proposals, and conducting successful editor/agent interviews. Along with her husband and children, she makes her home in the great state of Texas. To learn more, check out ElizabethLudwig.com or visit her on Facebook.

Fun Fact about
the Amish or Sugarcreek, Ohio

I was quite surprised during my recent wandering of Sugarcreek, Ohio, to see an Amish buggy approaching during a wet, cloudy day in mid-March. Though buggies are common in this part of Ohio, this one in particular was rigged with enough reflective tape to catch even the barest glimmer of light. Adding to the buggy's visibility was a set of extra-bright headlamps. I watched them in amazement as the buggy passed and was equally astounded to see an especially bright set of taillights shining from the rear. How was it possible? It wasn't until I got back to the hotel that I was let in on the secret.

Many Amish buggies come equipped with LED lights on the front and back that act as headlights, turn signals, and brake lights. They are either solar or battery powered and can last as long as one hundred hours on a single charge. While this may not be astounding to the average Englisher, it has proven quite a boon for these slower-moving vehicles and has more than likely saved countless number of lives.

SOMETHING DELICIOUS FROM OUR SUGARCREEK FRIENDS

Amish Cabbage Casserole

Amish Cabbage Casserole is an easy-to-make dish, yet it's hearty enough to satisfy any appetite!

1 medium green cabbage, cut into thin wedges
½ cup water
¼ cup butter or margarine
¼ cup all-purpose flour
2 cups milk
½ teaspoon salt
¼ teaspoon pepper
¾ cup cheddar cheese, shredded
½ cup mayonnaise
3 tablespoons chili sauce
½ cup finely chopped onion
½ cup green bell pepper, finely chopped

Preheat oven to 375 degrees.

Combine cabbage wedges and water in a large saucepan; cover and cook over medium heat for fifteen minutes. Drain well, and place cabbage wedges in a 12" × 8" × 2" dish.

Melt butter in a heavy saucepan over low heat; add flour, stirring until smooth. Cook over low heat for one minute, stirring constantly. Gradually add milk; cook over medium heat, stirring constantly, until mixture is thickened and bubbly. Stir in the salt and pepper. Pour mixture over cabbage, and bake at 375 degrees for twenty minutes.

Combine cheese, mayonnaise, chili sauce, onion, and green bell pepper; stir well and spread over cabbage. Bake at 400 degrees for twenty minutes.

Read on for a sneak peek of another exciting book
in the series Sugarcreek Amish Mysteries!

Blessed Are the Cheese Makers
by Tricia Goyer and Cara Putman

Red and silver ornaments swung from green garland, gracing the window of the Swiss Miss. The cold wind nipped at Cheryl's nose, and she tucked her scarf tight under her chin. Glancing back through the doorway, she watched Beau turn a slow circle on the Welcome mat.

"I'll be right back. I'm running to Swissters on a quick errand," she explained as if the cat could understand.

Both Lydia and Esther had arrived for what was sure to be a busy morning. Holiday shopping had begun in earnest last week with out-of-town visitors coming for Christmas in the Village, an annual candle-lighting ceremony to honor one of the town's local residents. She'd stood by Levi's side as, at the flip of a switch, the downtown area had come to life with beautiful tree and lighting displays. Even now her stomach warmed as she remembered how they'd sipped hot chocolate and listened to the strolling carolers. *If only I could feel truly at peace at Levi's side without worries of what others think of our friendship or frets over where this friendship will lead.*

Her black boots squeaked on the snow, and she turned her mind back to what she could be sure of. During the three weeks remaining before Christmas, the Swiss Miss and other Sugarcreek stores would be busier than ever. So would Cheryl as she managed the store, spent time with her friends, and prepared packages to send to her parents and brother.

The *clip-clop* of horses' hooves and buggy wheels mixed with the roar of truck engines as Cheryl crossed the street and then hurried down the road to Swissters. It was her favorite cheese shop in Sugarcreek. All of their cheese was made ten minutes away in Millersburg at Heini's Cheese Chalet. In the last year she'd sent gift baskets from here to family, and cheese would make the perfect gift for the wedding she would attend tomorrow.

The aroma of coffee filled the air as Cheryl entered Swissters. The coffee bar met her first and drew her in. She paused before it and scanned the holiday-decorated chalkboard listing the specials, and then she stepped back and shook her head.

"No, let me handle my shopping first, and then I'll get some coffee…," Cheryl mumbled, unwrapping the scarf from around her neck. A brisk Christmas tune played overhead.

She walked to the cheese display to choose some of her favorites. She was both nervous and excited about attending her first Amish wedding. She'd gotten to know Rhoda Hershberger over the last year as Rhoda brought in handmade items for the shop. She made the most beautiful lap quilts and Amish dolls. Before hearing about the wedding, Cheryl had sent Rhoda an especially big order for Rhoda to prepare for the Christmas season, and even with all the wedding planning, Rhoda had managed to fill the order.

Cheryl had many Amish-made gifts perfect for weddings, but Rhoda surely had a hope chest filled with those things. Then she'd remembered every new couple had a refrigerator to fill. She picked up an empty handbasket. A few other customers were also filling baskets with cheese and trying the samples. Cheryl already knew what most of them tasted like, but that didn't stop her from enjoying a few samples herself.

She had picked out a wheel of Colonel Cheddar and some garlic-and-herb yogurt cheese when the bell on the front door jingled. She turned, and a smile filled her face as Naomi entered. *Of all the people to run in to here.*

Naomi wore a heavy black coat over her Amish dress and apron and a bright red scarf. The pop of color made her cheeks glow—or maybe it was the cold air. Snow flecked the black bonnet that covered her *kapp.*

"Cheryl," Naomi called as she approached. "What a fun surprise to see you here. What are you up to?"

She held up the cheese. "Picking up some gifts. And you?"

"I'm here for a cup of coffee. I have already finished my morning errands. I could use something to keep me warm on the drive back to the farm."

"That's a good idea. I was thinking of getting a cup myself after my shopping."

"Oh, have you tried the olive pimento cheese?" Naomi reached into the chilled case and pulled out a small block. "I bought some the other day, and when I went to get some, Seth had gone through half of it for a snack. I should get more... and then hide it."

Cheryl chuckled, and a lightness filled her chest. "Are you sure it wasn't Levi who got into it?"

Naomi chuckled. "It could have been. The way the two of them eat. And Eli has recently tried to outdo them both. I believe he is going to pass Levi soon. He will be my gentle giant before he stops growing." Naomi shook her head with a grin. "Sometimes I think they all try to outdo each other."

"A healthy competition I suppose." Cheryl picked up a few more blocks of cheese and added them to the basket. "This should do it for me. If you need to go, I'll let you ring up your purchase first."

"*Ne*, I will walk to the counter with you. I am in no hurry. I only have chores waiting, and I do not mind if they wait longer."

LeeAnne Heath, the store owner, stood still behind the counter. Her head was lowered as if she were deep in thought. Her arms were crossed over her chest, and Cheryl was almost afraid to interrupt her pensiveness.

Cheryl placed her cheese on the counter. "It's sure cold out there."

LeeAnne glanced up and forced a smile. "Is this all today?"

"Well, I was hoping for this to be put into a gift basket and wrapped up..."

"Yes, of course." LeeAnne rang up the items, and Cheryl paid.

LeeAnne's brows furrowed. "Can I deliver the basket later today, Cheryl? I'm not sure if I'd do a very good job this morning."

"That's not a problem at all. It's for a wedding tomorrow." Cheryl was going to ask LeeAnne if she knew Rhoda then changed her mind. The woman didn't seem to be up for small talk today.

LeeAnne's fingers trembled slightly as Cheryl handed over the money. Tears rimmed the lower edges of her eyelids.

Cheryl tucked the change back into her wallet. *What's wrong with LeeAnne?* Should she pry?

Naomi paid for her block of cheese next. Her concerned glance settled on LeeAnne.

"Is everything all right, LeeAnne?" Cheryl asked.

LeeAnne brushed a strand of brown hair back from her face and let out a heavy sigh. "I'm waiting for a phone call. I've heard some...some horrible news..." The woman's lower lip trembled slightly.

Cheryl waited for the woman to say more, but LeeAnne pressed her lips into a tight line.

Naomi reached out her hand, placing it on LeeAnne's. "How can we help?"

Tears filled LeeAnne's eyes again and then spilled over from the outer corners of her eyes. She quickly wiped them away. "I don't know. I...I'm waiting to hear more. There was a fire this morning. My dad called to tell me."

Naomi gasped. "At your parents' house?"

"No. The cheese factory." LeeAnne covered her mouth with her hand. She shook her head in disbelief. "I haven't heard how bad, but Dad said things didn't look good. The production line may be down."

Naomi released a heavy sigh and pressed a hand to her heart. "Oh, I am so sorry."

Cheryl wondered what she could do to help. "Do you need to go to Millersburg? I can cover your store for you."

LeeAnne pointed to the back. "My assistant manager, Janelle, arrived. I heard her come in. I'm waiting for that phone call before I head down. But if you don't mind, I'm going back to check my cell phone—see if I received any more messages."

"We do not mind at all." Naomi pointed to the barista. "We are getting some coffee and will be here for a few minutes. Please let us know how we can help."

"Yes, of course." Then with a heavy sigh, LeeAnne hurried to the back room.

They walked to the espresso bar and ordered coffee, the happy Christmas music overhead now sounding too cheery.

"Maybe the fire is not as bad as it seems," Naomi offered. "I know all of us depend on Christmas sales to help us through the year...I imagine Heini's is no different."

"I sure hope it's not bad...but..." Cheryl pressed her upper teeth on her lower lip. "If the fire was on the production line, like LeeAnne believes, it can impact more than the holiday season... Who knows how long until they get their cheese production up and running again?"

"True. It is horrible, horrible."

A shuffling sounded behind Cheryl, and she turned. A young man stood there, tall and lanky with a scruffy blond beard. He picked up a jar of mustard off the shelf, but he seemed to be paying more attention to Cheryl than the item. He looked familiar in his oversize army jacket, ripped jeans, and Nike tennis shoes. His bedraggled blond hair stuck out from under a dirty baseball cap. Cheryl guessed she'd seen him around town. But the way he watched her...a chill traveled down Cheryl's spine, and for a moment she wished Levi were here too. One look at Levi's tall frame and broad shoulders and the young man wouldn't think about bothering her.

"What are Seth and Levi up to today?"

Naomi told her about the pruning Seth and Levi were doing around the farm. "Some of our neighbors like to prune their fruit trees in the spring, but my men are not much for sitting still. If there is a task to do, they will not sit around or put it off until later. But I imagine when Levi hears about the fire he will head down and help."

From behind Cheryl, footsteps neared. It was the young man, and she could hear his heavy breathing behind her. Goose bumps rose on her arms, and she clutched her purse tighter to her side. Surely he wouldn't try to steal her purse or grab her in the middle of a store, would he?

Naomi seemed oblivious to his presence. She smiled as she took her coffee from the barista's hands, but Cheryl couldn't get over the unsettled feeling. It was as if a hundred tiny ants crawled up her arms.

She quickly turned and saw he was still watching them. The young man flashed a nervous smile and then walked away. He moved to the long cooler display with all the cheese and leaned down as if intent on reading the labels.

Cheryl ordered next and paid for her coffee, leaving a generous tip. She was about to tell Naomi she'd walk her to her buggy when LeeAnne approached the counter again with the assistant manager by her side.

"So it's bad?" Janelle was asking.

"Worse than I thought. Dad said that I wouldn't recognize the production area. His phone was getting bad reception, and he's supposed to call me back on another phone, but from what I heard there's nothing that can be salvaged."

"Nothing?" A horrified look flashed across Janelle's face. "But what about...?"

The ringing of the store phone interrupted Janelle's words. Without hesitation LeeAnne picked it up. "Yeah, Dad. It's me." Then as she listened, the color drained from her face.

A Note from the Editors

We hope you enjoyed Sugarcreek Amish Mysteries, published by the Books and Inspirational Media Division of Guideposts, a nonprofit organization that touches millions of lives every day through products and services that inspire, encourage, help you grow in your faith, and celebrate God's love.

Thank you for making a difference with your purchase of this book, which helps fund our many outreach programs to military personnel, prisons, hospitals, nursing homes, and educational institutions.

We also create many useful and uplifting online resources. Visit Guideposts.org to read true stories of hope and inspiration, access OurPrayer network, sign up for free newsletters, download free e-books, join our Facebook community, and follow our stimulating blogs.

To learn about other Guideposts publications, including the best-selling devotional *Daily Guideposts*, go to Guideposts.org/Shop, call (800) 932-2145, or write to Guideposts, PO Box 5815, Harlan, Iowa 51593.